BenK

and the

UglY

PrincesS

BenK

and the

UglY
PrincesS

S.G. BYRD

Torchflame Books

Durham, NC

Copyright © 2021 Sarah G. Byrd
Benk and the Ugly Princess
S.G. Byrd
www.sgbyrd.com
sbyrd27514@gmail.com

Published 2021, by Torchflame Books
an Imprint of Light Messages Publishing
www.lightmessages.com
Durham, NC 27713 USA
SAN: 920-9298

Paperback ISBN: 978-1-61153-405-4
E-book ISBN: 978-1-61153-406-1
Library of Congress Control Number: 2020923985

To all those who have trouble believing
that the Maker loves them,
especially when they keep messing up

CONTENTS

ACKNOWLEDGMENTS

I am grateful to my husband, Bob Byrd, for helping me edit and make business decisions. His support has been a lifeline. Three other lifelines have continued to be my grandchildren—Ashley, Boaz, and Enoch Byrd, now ages 10, 9, and 7. Their enthusiasm for my stories has been tremendously encouraging. Love and appreciation to my children, Elizabeth, Stephen, and his wife Michelle, Sarah—and welcome to Will Wright, Sarah's fiancé, who likes my stories and honors me by comparing them to C.S. Lewis' *Narnia* series.

Betty and Wally Turnbull have published all three of the *Montaland* stories through Torchflame Books. It has been a joy and privilege to work with them.

Lane Mason has helped me get my social media accounts into order. I very much appreciate her hard work as my publicist!

Thanks to my editor, Meghan Bowker, who has made the story better.

My greatest acknowledgement goes to the Maker of all worlds, who called me to write fantasy and partnered with me in imagination, creativity, endurance, and practicality. Thank you for being my Senior Partner!

Chapter 1

BIRTH

Not all the kingdoms in Montaland, the mountain world, were happy ones.

When the newborn's wails broke the stillness, they expressed quite well the feelings of many people in the Kingdom of Yospaldo. The small group of women in the castle garden had been waiting for hours, however. They didn't want to cry; they wanted to sigh with relief. It was the ten-year-old boy standing behind the queen who had to scrunch up his face to keep from wailing along.

Queen Opal had seen him in a village a month ago. Not knowing any better, he'd smiled at the pretty lady. Not many children smiled at Opal. It had given her a good feeling.

"Who are you?" she'd asked, and the boy had answered, "Woofy." The funny name had made her laugh, another good sensation.

The boy had laughed when she laughed, and the attending courtiers had sniffed at his impudence. Woofy's father had run out of the General Store and put an arm around his son.

"S-sorry, your majesty. My boy's s-simple. He don't know any better."

The queen had tapped her chin, ignoring the man who wore the overalls of a common farmer.

"Woofy will be my new page. Bring him," she'd ordered

one of the courtiers.

Woofy had cried at leaving his father, but he'd learned that life at the palace meant punishment if he cried or did anything else that was considered wrong. He was simple but he learned. He wasn't happy but he adjusted.

This afternoon Opal had forgotten he was there. She lifted her hands and arranged her hair.

"It has been a trying day."

The other ladies murmured agreement.

"Narcissa will soon be running about the castle again, pretty as ever," a countess said with a trace of envy.

The new mother was Queen Opal's best friend. She was also the belle of the castle and the highest-ranking princess. Her husband had died shortly after she got pregnant, but he hadn't been as popular as his wife. Nobody had missed him, including Narcissa.

"Did she ever decide what to call the child?" asked one of the duchesses.

The queen laughed, remembering her friend's preoccupation with names.

"She narrowed it down to three and refused to let any of them go."

"It had better be a girl. She didn't choose any boy names," murmured the envious countess.

Opal arched her eyebrows.

"Of course it will be a girl. She will be an untouchable princess as beautiful as her mother, and we will marry her off at the age of sixteen. You forget yourself, Dannet."

Dannet started to apologize, but the queen froze her with a stare and turned away. That was when she caught sight of Woofy and remembered he was there.

"Go into the birthing house and bring me news. Don't they know I should be informed?"

Woofy found it hard to walk after standing for hours in one place. He tripped over his own feet and almost fell. The ladies laughed, but this time the boy didn't amuse the queen.

"Hurry," she said sharply.

Woofy ran as fast as he could up the steps of the birthing house. Opal rose from her chair and stretched. The minutes passed. She was frowning when the door of the birthing house opened again, but no doctor appeared to come apologetically down the steps. It was Woofy who shuffled into sight. He stood in the doorway, head hanging.

"I told you to hurry. If you don't come down those steps right now, you will be punished," she snapped.

Woofy came, but he was dragging his feet, and the queen's face set in hard lines. He stopped in front of her.

"They s-s-said s-s-sorry," he stammered.

Opal's face paled. "What? How is Narcissa?"

"N-not good. She dead."

Queen Opal stood motionless. The ladies around her held their breaths, afraid to make any sound that would draw attention to them.

"Get away from me," Opal finally said in an unnatural voice, and when Woofy didn't move right away, she pushed him hard and kicked him when he fell. "I never want to see you again," she hissed.

Woofy scrambled out of reach on his hands and knees. Lurching to his feet, he ran toward the front gate. His arm had scraped on a rock as he fell, and his side hurt where he'd been kicked, but his face was beaming. He could go home now. Someone would give him a ride if they were going that way, but if he had to walk, he would.

The queen stalked up the steps, into the house, and down the hall, but she stopped two steps into the birthing room. A still form covered with a sheet lay on the bed in front of her. That couldn't be Narcissa, pretty vivacious Narcissa. Narcissa wouldn't lie there without moving. She would be demanding attention—and getting it too.

The queen pressed her lips together and went over to the bed. With one hand, she drew back the sheet. Her friend's beautiful face lay on the pillow. Her eyes had been closed, but whoever closed them had been in too much of a hurry to do a good job. One eye was slightly open. With a shudder, Queen Opal pulled the sheet back over the white features.

A cry came from the next room, and Opal started as if she'd been slapped. The baby was alive! With purposeful steps, she opened the door that connected the two rooms and stalked over to the edge of a crib heavily decorated with pink silk ribbons and eight-inch-wide swaths of lace.

A middle-aged woman sat beside the crib. Knowing well what the queen's reaction to him would be, the doctor had left right after Narcissa died. His assistants had left with him. Only the baby's nurse had dared to remain.

Opal's face convulsed as she stared at the red-faced wailing infant.

"That is the ugliest baby I have ever seen. Why is it crying?"

"She'll stop soon, your Majesty. It's her way of going to sle—"

"A girl," Opal interrupted bitterly. "The baby girl that was to be the best plaything Narcissa and I ever had. Take her out of here. I don't want her."

The nurse rose and started gathering baby items together.

"I hate that baby. I hate her," screamed the queen.

Opal didn't often lose control. She liked to stay calm and regal. "One must take life's stings as if they don't matter. Gaiety in the face of misfortune shows strength of character!"

When she did lose control, however, she lost it completely.

The nurse grabbed the baby girl from her cradle and ran through the front door. As she passed the small group of women, she motioned toward the house. The queen's hysterical screams could be heard quite plainly.

"You'd better take care of her," she told them before hurrying off.

The women stayed right where they were, exchanging glances that silently agreed. Let Queen Opal get over the first violence of her reaction before they entered. Then they would get credit for comforting her instead of blame for being present when the sad event happened.

The queen's grief lasted five days, during which time she either lay in bed and moaned, or huddled in her favorite chair and wept. The fifth day, she put on a blue velvet, party dress and smiled when one of the massive full-length mirrors in the royal bedroom revealed that she had lost weight during her time of mourning. Sweeping into the massive throne room, she ordered a banquet and dance for the evening.

"Narcissa would want us to," she said dramatically.

The King of Yospaldo rose to stand at his wife's side. The court ladies touched their eyes with perfumed handkerchiefs, while the men lowered their gaze respectfully. Everyone was pleased.

The palace began to hum again.

Servants scurried around preparing food and setting up decorations for the party. Nobility dashed about comparing clothes and gossiping over dance partners. The queen graciously forgave Woofy. She sent a courier to his father's farm to bring him back to the castle. He didn't want to come, but what difference did that make?

The baby was completely forgotten.

"That's right, come to Nurse Broomely," urged the nurse tenderly.

The baby girl pulled herself up again and held onto the old kitchen chair. Her chubby face beamed. This was a fun game. She liked it.

"You can do it. Try again."

Slowly the eleven-month-old moved first one foot and then the other. The nurse held her breath. She was walking. The toddler moved awkwardly forward, her face wreathed in smiles, and the older woman caught and hugged her.

"Remember what this letter says?" Nurse Broomely asked, pointing to a "c."

"C-c-c, like a squirrel when you bother it," said the -year-old girl sitting at her desk.

"Don't chew your ponytail," her nurse corrected automatically. "Now what does the next letter say?"

"A-a-a-a, like a goat!"

"That's right! Now the last one; what does it say?"

The girl placed her tongue behind her front teeth. "T-t-t, like you, Nurse B, when you're scolding me!"

Nurse Broomely chuckled but refused to be sidetracked. "Put them together and what do they say?"

The little girl bent over her paper and concentrated. The end of her black ponytail crept back into her mouth. "C-c-c-a-a-a-t-t-t," she sounded out. "C-c-a-a-t-t; oh, it says 'cat,' doesn't it? Cat!"

The two goats lifted their heads and bleated. The eleven-year-old had startled them when she jumped down from the tree, but they knew her. She milked them daily and rubbed behind their ears. They went back to eating the tender spring grass.

Moodily she watched them. Why couldn't she ever talk to people in the village? Nurse Broomely was mean! When her dog came bounding through the pasture, barking with excitement at having found her, she frowned. Ruff was always with her. She had sneaked up to the goat pasture to have some time by herself. The little dog raced around the tree in a frenzy of joy, and her frown couldn't help but fade at his antics. Besides, twilight was her favorite time of day, especially in the summer. The heat of the afternoon had passed, but the cold of a mountain night had not yet come. The goats wandered purposefully down toward the barn. They wanted to be milked. She would have to go too.

Reluctantly she walked through the pasture. A short

distance from the gate, she paused and leaned against a tree. There was so much to think about but never time to do it, even with no friends to distract her. No friends. The girl tried to get angry again but wound up sagging against the tree. She knew why Nurse Broomely wouldn't let her have friends. People from court mustn't hear about her. They might take her away. It was just too hard.

The dusk deepened. Then a warm light glowed in the window of the cottage below her. Nurse Broomely would be calling soon. With a sigh the girl pushed away from the trunk of the tree. Her movement startled three deer that had been passing silently through the pasture. They bounded off in great leaps. Growling ferociously, Ruff wanted to chase them, but she held him back. How graceful the deer were! How could they jump that high?

Nurse Broomely leaned out the cottage door. The girl could see her silhouette against the light. It was a round silhouette—pleasantly plump, her nurse insisted. Taking a big breath, the girl bounded through the pasture, pretending to be a deer. She felt as if she were flying. Her dog thought it was a race and ran all out to beat her.

Laughing, she scrambled over the gate instead of opening it and ran to the cottage.

"Why do I have to learn court etiquette? I live in a cottage. I take care of two goats and one dog! They don't need me to curtsey to them!"

Nurse Broomely exhaled heavily. "I'm afraid the Yospaldon court will remember you one day. These are the things you might need to know if you ever have to—"

"Don't say it! I'll never leave you," insisted the fourteen-year-old, shaking her head so vehemently her long black braids whipped from side to side.

The old nurse's eyes took on a far-away look as she responded. "The Maker is the only one who can say that. He will never leave us."

"I know. But I love you."

Nurse Broomely focused on her again.

"I love you too, child. That's why I want you to learn these things. Now try it again, bending more at the waist."

———— ∞∞ ————

When the noblemen came, the girl was caught unawares. She had been kneading bread, and her apron was covered with flour. The two men rode their horses up the rutted driveway in front of a carriage that rattled contemptuously over the bumps.

Nurse Broomely went to talk to them, holding the door as if she didn't want them to come in, but she was a peasant. The men pushed her aside and searched the cottage until they found the girl with flour on her hands. They laughed at the sight, but their laughter didn't stop them from demanding that she come with them.

Numbly the girl took off her apron and brushed the flour off her hands. At the same time her head rose with determination. She had planned what to say if this ever happened.

"I will go," she announced.

The men laughed again. What a presumptuous chit!

"But I will take my nurse with me."

She lifted her nose and stared at the men from the Yospaldon court through eyes that had grown cold and compelling. Nurse Broomely was horrified at her arrogance; however, these men were just noblemen. They didn't rank nearly as high as a princess, and that was what this young chit was, for all her flour. A princess of the Yospaldon court turned cold and compelling several times a day. If her wishes weren't obeyed, there were immediate and painful consequences for whoever had annoyed her.

"Certainly, Princess," and "as you will, Princess," became the order of the day.

Nurse Broomely had also prepared for this day. She and the girl went upstairs to change clothes and throw a few more things into the bags that had been packed and repacked for years as the girl had grown. When they came back down, they were escorted to the carriage. The men even agreed to stop at a neighbor's farm so Nurse Broomely could give them the goats and chickens.

"I'm glad Ruff died last month. He wouldn't have liked it away from the farm."

The girl's voice quivered and Nurse Broomely reached for her hand. Hours later, they were still holding hands as the carriage drove into the castle grounds.

Chapter 2

BLOTCHES

Princess Pearlrope Diamonde Primrose peered intently into the bathroom mirror. There was a Welcome to Spring Reception in the courtyard that morning, and she wanted to make sure she looked right.

Picking up a bottle, she squeezed a drop of pus onto the end of a stick and dabbed it close to her nose. There—it was in place but it would ooze down her cheek unless—quickly she squirted red liquid from another bottle over the pus. It dried instantly, holding the pus on her cheek but letting a little dribble from the top. A perfect blotch!

"One of my best," she said with satisfaction, studying it from all angles in the obliging mirror.

Mirrors were everywhere in the Yospaldon palace. Any side room could be counted on to have them. The ladies-in-waiting, countesses, duchesses, and princesses often wanted to check on their elaborate hairstyles or put more color on their faces. The courtiers, dukes, and earls weren't above doing the same thing.

"Rose, are you ready?"

The princess smiled. She dipped a comb in grease and ran it through her hair. Then she left the bathroom.

"How do you like my new blotch?"

Nurse Broomely nodded her approval.

"Very sickening! Here's your middle."

Rose lifted her arms and let the older woman wrap a flesh-colored tube around her waist.

"It stinks," she remarked, wrinkling her nose.

Nurse Broomely paused.

"Not too much, I hope. If we overdo it, your disguise might be exposed."

"It's not too much. I have a feel for what I can get by with now."

"That's my girl," said the nurse before a racking cough bent her over.

"That cough's been dragging on. Why don't you take a nap this afternoon," Rose suggested.

Nurse Broomely muttered something the girl couldn't hear and helped her pull on the dress they had chosen for the reception. It was a drab shade of gold with bright purple flowers on the sleeves and neckline. The purple accented the various blotches on Rose's face and the gold dulled her skin tone.

"I look awful!" she said, spinning lightly around in front of the floor-length mirror in her bedroom.

Nurse Broomely shook her head.

"Too graceful."

"I was thinking of putting a blotch on my neck."

"You're already late," her nurse pointed out and shooed her out the door. "Be sure and let people see you're there. I'll be praying." Rose's face brightened. She lifted her face and whispered her own prayer as she waddled down the hall. Stopping in front of the door that led outside, she practiced a few sneezes. No good, they were too normal.

Well, she could always burp.

With that, Rose pushed through the door into a courtyard full of people. Several men stood near the door, laughing and twirling their mustaches on their fingers.

"Sure, sure, you climbed up to the timberline," one of

them said, snorting in disbelief. "How many wedewolves did you jump over?"

"I didn't count," the young man with the biggest mustache answered nonchalantly.

His friends laughed and he smirked at them.

"Use your heads, idiots; it was broad daylight. Wedewolves hunt at night. You wouldn't catch me anywhere near the timberline at night. It took a lot of courage to go as high as I did in the middle of the day, but I wanted that arrow. It had sentimental value. Cecilia kissed it."

He winked, implying that Cecilia had kissed other things as well.

His friends snickered appreciatively, but their attention was still on the wedewolves.

"I've heard they have orange eyes without pupils. They never give up on a hunt, though nothing can run from them long. Their howls are so terrifying the prey becomes paralyzed with fear. It doesn't even feel the first bite." Rose had paused to listen. The wedewolves of the high mountain range behind the palace fascinated her. Everyone in Yospaldo was afraid of them and rarely went near the timberline. That was the very reason she was interested in them. If she and Nurse Broomely ever escaped—"

"Phew! What is that smell?"

She stiffened. Rose was short and could go unnoticed for a couple of minutes, but she'd waited too long this time. The men had spotted her. They backed away, gagging.

"It's our dear Pearlrope," one of them called in a shrill falsetto.

"No, no, no, you've got it wrong. It's our very royal Princess Diamond! Untouchable, you know."

Yospaldons have one name—one! Why did my mother give me three?

She knew the answer. She had been told many times since she came to the Yospaldon court that her mother hadn't been able to choose between her favorite names.

Accustomed to receiving everything she wanted, Narcissa had treated her baby accordingly and given the yet unborn child every name she liked.

I hate my names, all but Primrose, and I only like that when Nurse B shortens it to Rose.

"Kiss her," someone called to the young man with the big mustache. "They wouldn't punish you. You're too brave. Tickle her with your favorite arrow. She'll give it sentimental value."

That was going too far. The young man's face hardened.

"Shut up. I'd as soon kiss the rear end of a pig."

A chorus of laughter followed this witty comparison. Rose took advantage of it to lose herself in the crowd around the food tables.

"WHAT DO YOU MEAN BY TOUCHING ME?"

Oh no.

Unwittingly, Rose had bumped against one of the two people in the Yospaldon court she tried hardest to avoid. The young woman next to her had long blonde hair roped artistically around her face. Her dress was cut low to expose as much of her breasts as was considered fashionable for that time of day. She was holding a shapely arm to one side as if it had been exposed to a plague.

"Answer me. How do you dare touch me, filth?"

Rose took a deep breath and let it out again in Goldsheen's direction. It didn't work. She had forgotten to chew a garlic pod this morning. *I'll have to talk my way out of this one.*

Princess Goldsheen had a terrible temper and invariably lost it when she came near Rose. More than anything else, she hated the fact that the two of them shared the status of untouchable princesses.

"What's the matter? Goldsheen, is anyone bothering you?" a deep female voice asked.

Rose cringed. The voice belonged to the second person in Yospaldo that she made every effort to avoid.

Goldsheen fluttered her long lashes. "It's Pearlrope, your

Majesty. She deliberately bumped against my arm. I think she's trying to ruin my complexion."

Queen Opal's cold glance raked across Rose's face before she turned back to Goldsheen.

"Don't make such a fuss, Princess. It is not possible to ruin someone's complexion by touch. You must try to get along better with Pearlrope. These frequent outbursts are annoying. She is ugly and you are beautiful; nevertheless, you are both untouchable princesses."

Goldsheen frowned at the reminder, but she knew better than to argue with the queen, who was continuing her monologue.

"It is true that you were raised in the palace while Pearlrope grew up in a common hut, but we corrected that mistake as soon as we remembered it had been made. Each of you will be married after your sixteenth birthday. We have not had an untouchable princess marry for quite some time. Noblemen will pay any amount to obtain one of you for a wife."

The queen finished her speech and started to leave, but then stopped and looked again at Rose.

What do I do? If it had been anyone else, she would have made one of the prolonged burps that she had perfected with practice, but she couldn't burp in the queen's face.

"How old are you, Pearlrope?"

"Fourteen," Rose said, trying to hold her breath.

Prolonged burps were useful, but the skill had come with a drawback. Burping had become an automatic response to tense situations. She could feel one building up inside of her now and tried hard to squelch it. A hiccup was the result.

The queen responded slowly. "Ah yes, fourteen. We have an interested suitor coming to meet Goldsheen soon. We will present you to him also."

"A suitor! Who is he?" Goldsheen squealed with excited pleasure.

"Prince Pamsby," the queen answered, never taking her

eyes off Rose's face.

Dim memories of a red-faced man who drank too much and leered at the servant girls flitted through Rose's mind. *I'd rather die.*

"He will have to choose between the two of you," Opal finished smoothly.

Despite their fear of the queen, the courtiers around them laughed. Choose between beautiful Goldsheen and repulsive Pearlrope—what kind of choice was that?

Goldsheen simpered.

"There is more to Pearlrope than you know," Queen Opal reproved.

The laughter immediately stopped. At the same time, Rose's mouth fell open and an enormous burp surged out. The queen smiled a little, emboldening the crowd to laugh again.

"The years pass, don't they, Pearlrope? We will see that you look your best when Pamsby is here," she said coldly as she moved away.

Oh no! her mind shrieked, and her heart jumped out of its proper location and jammed into her throat. Frantic to get away, she pushed through the crowd. People jumped to the side obligingly, holding their noses and sometimes making gagging noises, but laughing, always laughing. Rose was accustomed to being ridiculed and could generally brush it off, but right now she felt vulnerable. The laughter stung like lashes from a hundred whips.

She ran across the courtyard and into one of the castle doors. It wasn't possible to return to her rooms, which were always cleaned that time of day. The Yospaldon court would be horrified if a princess stayed when the servants were cleaning—and the castle servants would be sure to let them know. Rose made a quick decision. The cellar wouldn't be in use, and she could get more of the dried food she'd been smuggling from the castle in case she and Nurse Broomely escaped.

How much does Queen Opal know?

The cellar was located near the kitchen, toward the back of the castle. Servers panted through the halls, carrying the large trays of food that would replenish what was being eaten at the reception. They didn't pay any attention to the girl who waddled silently past them.

She waited by the door to the cellar, pretending to adjust a shoe while another server came out of the kitchen. If he saw her going into the cellar, he'd tell on her in a minute. None of the castle staff could be trusted—but then she saw his round face. Poor Woofy, everyone made fun of him. Rose knew he'd been at the castle for years in an off and on pattern. He had grown to be six feet tall but was still a boy at heart. Whenever he did something especially stupid, he'd be sent home, but the queen invariably called him back.

It's cruel. She knows he'd rather stay home.

Rose gave him a half-smile. Woofy usually smiled back, but this time he didn't see her. His lips were parted and his tongue was poking out. The tray he was carrying was so overloaded that he had to concentrate on keeping it level. The kitchen staff was probably hoping he'd drop it and get into trouble.

As soon as Woofy passed, Rose opened the door and darted into the cellar. It was dark, but she'd learned her way around and hurried down the steps without any problem. When she got to the cellar floor, she weaved through the barrels to the corner reserved for dried foods. Normally she brought a bag tied on the inside of her dress. She'd fill the bag with packets of food and then fasten her dress around it. Another bulge or so didn't really matter. This time she wasn't as well prepared. Her false middle could hold a couple of packets though, and Rose stuffed one into it. She was reaching for another when the cellar door opened and closed.

Oh no, her mind shrieked again, and she crouched behind

the nearest barrel. Someone was coming down the steps; two someones from the number of footsteps. They didn't seem to want a light any more than she did. A giggle escaped one of them.

Goldsheen? In the cellar? Rose wanted to peek around the barrel, but she didn't dare move from her uncomfortable crouch.

"Over here," a man whispered.

There were more giggles. Then there was a long pause, punctuated by what sounded more like slurping than kissing. Rose eased herself down until she was sitting on the floor. This could take a while.

The next few minutes seemed to stretch into hours. The cellar floor was cold and she wrapped her arms around her legs, hoping she wouldn't sneeze. By the time the couple left the cellar, Rose was so disgusted she wanted to throw up. She stuffed a second packet of dried food into her middle and slipped out of the cellar. Then she went back through the castle, heading for the stable this time and her hidden backpack.

The Welcome to Spring Reception was drawing to a close, though most of the people were still there. She would have to walk past them to get to the stable. Rose didn't feel ready to handle the Yospaldon court again, but she steeled herself. She'd skipped several things recently and it would be good for her to be seen. Nurse Broomely would be pleased.

There was a packed crowd around the food tables with small groups of two or three people talking and laughing along its edges. Rose waddled as inconspicuously as possible, but it was no use.

"Oh my, there goes—" a woman started and the crowd joined in eagerly, "Princess Pearlrope Diamond Primrose." They finished in a torrent of loud laughter.

The smell of food was Rose's undoing. She hadn't eaten since yesterday's lunch, because she'd missed last night's seven-course meal to find cough medicine for Nurse

Broomely. Breakfast hadn't been served that morning due to the Welcome to Spring Reception. She felt weak with hunger, and the crowd's laughter was having its whiplash effect again. In her haste to get away, she stumbled and fell to her knees. That prompted a fresh wave of laughter. Several tears made their embarrassing way down her cheeks.

Not yet. Hold it in.

As quickly as she could waddle, she passed the reception. A grassy slope led her down to the main stable, a beautiful building that showed the rest of the mountain world how highly Yospaldons regarded their horses. Rose walked through the big front doors and checked out the central aisle. No one was there, so she hurried through the barn to the storage stall that held halters, lead ropes, and saddle blankets—not the fancy ones, but the ones for everyday use. There was an old jump in one of the back corners. A few horse blankets hung over it, but they weren't the easiest to reach and were rarely used.

Dropping to her hands and knees, Rose crawled under the blankets. At the end of the stall, she pushed a loose board to one side and wiggled past it into a narrow corridor that ran between the stalls and the back wall of the stable. It was her favorite place to hide. As long as no one saw her enter, she was perfectly safe—unless she made too much noise.

Rose didn't get far before breaking down. She lowered her head into her hands and cried, rocking back and forth as she tried not to make any noise. Her head hurt by the time she got herself under control, but she had to make herself think.

Queen Opal knows too much. It had been a bad day in many respects, but that unexpected revelation had been the worst part, with Prince Pamsby's upcoming visit a close second. *We have to leave right away, but how?* It was more an expression of desperation than a question, but to her surprise, an answer popped into her mind.

The Maker will take care of us, child. And that is that!

Rose's fear ebbed a little at the reminder of Nurse Broomely's familiar, no-nonsense statement. *But how? How can we leave this place? Maker, you've got to do something! We're trapped here. We're trapped!*

Was this prayer or panic? Rose tried to pull herself together.

He's watched over us until now, she told herself a little doubtfully. *At least I didn't have to grow up in the Yospaldon court. And Nurse Broomely was allowed to return to the palace when I had to come back. I don't know how I would've handled life here without her.*

Anxious as she was, Rose couldn't help but smile slightly as she remembered those first few months at court. Everyone had whispered about her. Even the outlying farms had heard the sad truth. It had been regrettable, very regrettable, but also undeniable that the new untouchable princess couldn't handle the rich food of the upper class. Her face had broken out and she'd steadily gained weight. Nothing the other women advised or suggested had made any difference. They'd eventually given up, shrugging their shoulders.

Queen Opal could have commanded her to eat differently, but that would have involved noticing her. The queen had brought the princess to court for financial reasons only. An untouchable princess was too valuable a commodity not to exploit. Opal had ordered rooms prepared for her and let it be known that she expected the new princess to be given the prestige due her unique position, but that had been it. She hadn't greeted Rose or spoken to her when they passed in the halls. As far as possible, the queen had ignored the existence of the girl who had offended her at birth.

"I'm untouchable. Why work so hard to make myself ugly?" Rose had asked at first.

"You don't want to know. Just do as I say," had been Nurse Broomely's reply, and soon the whole thing had become a game—how ugly could Rose get and still come across as genuine. She hadn't questioned Nurse Broomely again. Living day after day in the castle, she'd seen for herself what the place was like. The morning calls of the birds had mixed with screams from people in the dungeon. Farmers and tradesmen selling their wares had to take what was offered or get thrown out of the palace without wares or payment.

"We've got to leave this place," Rose said out loud in the empty corridor behind the horse stalls and was immediately appalled at herself.

No more noise. Someone might discover this hiding place. Wiping her cheeks, she crawled forward until she reached her backpack with its two blankets, two hammocks, and dried food. Her stomach grumbled when she stored the new packets of food, but it wouldn't be a good idea to eat any of the precious supplies

We'll need them--I hope.

There wasn't room to turn around in the narrow corridor, but Rose had become an expert at crawling backwards. When she reached the loose boards, she started to maneuver through them into the storage stall. Halfway through, she froze in place. Behind the old jump where nobody could see it from the stall, but where she couldn't miss it on her way out, was a turkey sandwich wrapped in a piece of paper. On top of the paper someone had drawn the crude shape of a fish, the ancient symbol of the Maker's people. The earliest settlers had brought the knowledge of him from their old world and taught their children about him. Those children had grown up and taught their own children, and so it had passed on. *And Nurse Broomely taught me.* Rose grabbed the sandwich and took a big bite. *Pickles,* she thought happily and then ate too fast to think any further.

After her meal, she crawled past the jump and stood up. The paper with the fish drawn on it was in her pocket. She couldn't wait to show it to Nurse Broomely. It was too bad she couldn't go back to their rooms right away. They were probably clean by now, but she didn't want to walk past that horrible reception again.

Besides, she was thirsty. Those pickles had been unusually salty. She needed something to drink right away, and the nearest source of water was the stable pump. A few workers were cleaning stalls and calling back and forth to each other, but when she peeked out of the storage stall, no one was in sight. Making herself waddle just in case, she reached the side door leading to the pump without incident.

Rose stepped into the sunlight with relief—and stopped short.

A large bearded man stood by the pump as if waiting on someone. A bucket of water was next to him, and as Rose slipped back into the shade of the door, she expected him to pick it up and leave. She willed him to leave, preferably in a different direction. He would yell at her if he saw her. He yelled at everybody, even the nobility. If he hadn't been such an expert with horses, they would never have put up with it, but the master of the Yospaldon stable could get by with a lot. Yospaldons prided themselves on their well-trained horses.

The master glanced around. When he saw her in the shadow of the door, he grabbed the bucket and stomped into the stable right past her. He didn't yell. He didn't even look at her after that first identifying glance, but as he passed the shrinking girl, he muttered, "Tonight, after dark."

Rose had no idea what he meant. Why hadn't he yelled at her? She went to the pump and got a long drink of water. Then she waddled to the nearest fence. Several horses grazing in the pasture lifted their heads at her approach. A golden palomino wandered over for a closer look. Picking a handful of green grass on her side of the fence, Rose offered it to him. He took it greedily and searched the ground for the pieces that fell.

"It's the same grass you have on your side, silly," she said and watched him wander off again.

She liked horses, though her riding was below average compared to the other Yospaldons. Even the laziest court ladies worked at their riding techniques. Rose could have cared less how her fingers should hold the reins and where her elbows were supposed to be. She was always near the bottom of the monthly rankings. It was true though that living in the castle had meant she could be around beautiful horses.

That's one good thing. And learning how to embroider is another.

Her skill for creating pictures with a needle and thread was exceptional. Nurse Broomely had worried it would draw attention to her, but embroidery wasn't highly regarded in Yospaldo. There were no rankings for it. It was simply something high-born ladies should know how to do.

Rose wished she could go embroider right now, but since that was impossible, she leaned on the fence and dreamed of leaping onto the palomino's back and galloping away. It didn't matter where they went—as long as it was away from Yospaldo.

Sure. As if I'd ever leave Nurse B!

When a loud bell rang twice, she straightened gladly. The reception was over. That afternoon there was a court session in which the King would settle disputes. An elaborate feast was planned for the evening. Nurse Broomely wanted her to go to both events. If she didn't, someone might notice—but right now she could return to their rooms.

Rose waddled fast. She had news to share, and it burst out as soon as she saw her nurse.

"At the entrance to my secret tunnel, someone left a sandwich wrapped in paper that had a fish drawn on it. Here it is; I saved it for you to see. I don't know who left it."

The old nurse started to speak, but Rose was too wound up to let her say anything. Everything burst out at once.

"There's a suitor coming. Queen Opal asked how old I

was and when I told her fourteen, she said there was more to me than people know, so she must suspect I have a disguise. She's going to make the suitor choose between Goldsheen and me. He'll choose her, of course, but the Queen wants me to look my best. That way, she can raise the marriage price. Goldsheen was delighted with the whole thing, but while I was getting more packets of dry food, she snuck into the cellar with a man! Can you believe it? I stayed hidden, but it was the most disgusting thing I've ever heard. I felt like throwing up! How could they do such a thing? She's untouchable. Don't they know the penalty for even one kiss?"

Rose stopped for breath, and Nurse Broomely finally had a chance to respond. She had taken the paper with the fish drawn on it, but she didn't mention it. Instead she responded to Rose's last question.

"They know—a severe beating and banishment from court."

"Then why—"

"They're not happy, child. None of them are. They try to find fulfilment in the places that are allowed and don't find it. Then they try the places that aren't allowed. An untouchable princess means a young girl who's touched in secret. That's the only difference."

Rose stared at her.

"That's why you made me ugly. I thought you just didn't want me to fit in, but it was more than that, wasn't it?"

"Do you remember the times men grabbed at you even though you were ugly?" Nurse Broomely asked, holding a hand over her mouth to stop a cough. "It could have been much worse!"

The cough came with a vengeance then. It was obvious that Nurse Broomely wanted to say more, but every time she tried, she had a coughing spell.

The bell rang, announcing the afternoon court session. Rose had to leave, but as she hurried to the door, she told her nurse, "Take a nap. I'll get more medicine after the law court."

Her nurse held back a cough with superhuman effort.

"No. Come back here."

"Okay," Rose said and then hurried off. She would be late as it was.

Chapter 3

Escape

R ose shifted positions in her seat. The unlucky countess next to her gagged slightly, covering her nose and sliding away as far as possible.

The court session dragged on, interesting nobody. Who cared which of those wealthy farmers owned the small field they were haggling over! It didn't matter what they said in any case. Their bribes had been received, and whoever had offered the most money would get the field. Rose didn't know why the King let them keep talking. Maybe it made him feel important. At last even he reached his limit.

"Enough! I have made my decision. The field goes to Farmer Bludgett."

Both farmers left without saying a word. The one who had lost was disappointed over losing both the field and the money he would never see again, even though it had not been the highest bribe. The winner was wishing he had offered less on his bribe. Maybe he would have still won. There were sour expressions on both their faces.

To everyone's relief, the next case was the last one scheduled for that afternoon. Rose tuned out the initial explanations and desperately tried to come up with a plan. The queen could command at any moment that Rose throw off her disguise. She'd be forced to start the beautifying rituals that Goldsheen was undoubtedly eager to do. Yospaldons knew all kinds of ways to make themselves more attractive. Her skin would be softened with rich oils. Her hair would be made silky with goat's milk and herbs. Her freedom of movement would be taken away. She'd be trapped.

Rose moved restlessly in her chair. She and Nurse Broomely had to leave Yospaldo, but even if they managed to escape, where would they go? Where would they live? She was frowning hard when something unexpected happened. The case ended. Neither of the complainants had shown up. After decreeing that they both be fined for wasting the time of the court, the king stood. Rose jumped to her feet with everyone else and waited impatiently as the queen rose in a smooth graceful movement to stand beside the king. The royal couple paced grandly out of the room.

Rose was the next out of the door. Waddling at high speed, she navigated the twists and turns of the castle, sped down her hall, and entered her room again at last.

"Nurse B, where are you?"

There was no answer. That was unusual. Nurse Broomely was usually in their rooms, and she had told Rose to come back after the law court.

She's taking a nap, but the thought made her feel uneasy. Nurse Broomely didn't like resting during the day.

"I don't have time to nap. I'll save it for the high home," she'd say crustily.

Crossing the large sitting room, Rose peeked into the smaller of the two bedrooms. Yes, her nurse was there under a blanket. Nurse B must have laid down that afternoon, sick as she was, and fallen asleep. Rose started to close the door, but a harsh cough from the bed stopped her. Flying across the room, she leaned over her old friend. The older woman had no energy left, but the cough tore at her throat again and again, until she sank back exhausted on her pillow.

Rose ran to get a glass of cold water. It had helped in the past. She brought it to her nurse's lips, but the older woman took one sip and refused any more. Her eyes were on Rose, and they had the anxious expression Rose knew all too well.

"Go child, tonight." The words fluttered out of the sick woman's throat.

"What? I'm not going anywhere without you."

Rose spoke in her firmest, most stubborn manner, but Nurse Broomely gave her head the slightest shake.

"Ricaldo will help—at stable."

"I've never heard of him," Rose objected , frowning at the very idea of accepting help from any Yospaldon. A ghost of a smile passed over Nurse Broomely's face.

"Master—the fish."

Rose had no time to let that bit of news register in her mind. Another spell of wrenching coughs hit the nurse's body. Somebody groaned deeply, and Rose had no idea whether she was the one who had groaned or Nurse Broomely. There were tears on both their faces. When the coughing spell passed, the older woman's body lay motionless.

"No," Rose said and frantically felt for a pulse in the wrist, the neck.

There was nothing. Shaking all over as if she had a high fever, Rose sank onto the floor. She didn't know how long she stayed there. Voices from the sitting room aroused her at last.

"How can we wash and dress the filthy thing if we can't find her?" a woman was saying.

Rose heard the words but was too dulled by pain to think what they might mean. It wasn't any particular sense of danger that made her crawl past the edges of the old blanket into the darkness under the bed. She just didn't want to be disturbed.

Leave me alone.

Clacking shoes moved to the other side of the sitting room and were muted briefly by the lush rug in Rose's bedroom.

"She's not in her room. We'll get blamed if she's not

presentable—you know we will."

The words got louder as the shoes clacked back across the sitting room to the door of Nurse Broomely's small room.

"Get up!" came the angry command.

There was no rug in the nurse's room. The shoes clacked across the floor. Then there was a loud scream and a flurry of commotion outside Rose's dark haven. It seemed removed from her, as if it were happening miles away to someone else. Her head dropped onto her arms in misery.

Eventually she slept.

When she woke up, the blanket that had shielded her from the rest of the world was gone. Cautiously moving to the edge of the bed, she peered out. Night had come. The windows were open, and the curtains Nurse Broomely had made moved with the breezes that pushed into the room. It must have rained while she'd slept. The air smelled fresh.

Rose revived enough to crawl from under the bed and stand up. Then a high note of distress escaped her. Her friend's body was gone. The bed had been stripped of sheets as well as blanket, and the dirty, stained mattress that was left didn't look like Nurse Broomely, who was always tidy and clean.

"I was sleeping. They took her while I was sleeping," Rose whispered tearfully, but she didn't have time for grief. She had to obey Nurse Broomely's last request.

I need something to take with me.

Pulling open the top drawer of her nurse's old chest, Rose felt a deep surge of relief. The drawers had not been emptied. Nurse Broomely's undergarments were there, too worn and patched to interest the Yospaldon court. Not even the other servants would want them. There was an old sachet in their midst that Rose had embroidered when she was first learning how to make the different stitches. Two goats were looking at a barking puppy. The animals' shapes were crude and the embroidery stitches were far from perfect, but her talent could be seen even at that early stage. The fat little puppy was brimming with mischief; the goats looked both curious and suspicious at the same time. Nurse Broomely had liked it.

Rose's eyes were beginning to sting with tears again. She picked up the sachet and dropped it into the front of her dress. It would be safely held in place by her fake middle.

An old blue scarf was folded neatly in a corner of the bottom drawer. Nurse Broomely had worn it often. Rose held the soft wool in her arms as if it were a living thing. She turned and stared one more time at the empty room. A gusty wind full of rain smells blew through the window, making her jump. Quickly she threw the blue scarf around her neck and knotted it loosely.

Then she crept from the bedroom and through the sitting room. The hall was dark and deserted. Where was everyone? Of course—they were at the feast; the one Rose had planned to go to, though she hated those long drawn-out meals. She was glad of them now. For at least three hours, the whole palace would be busy; servants and nobles alike. Rose went down the hall and out into the wet night, heading toward the stable.

There were a few workers in the stable; she could hear them whistling. Rose was standing under a tree near the entrance when a big man came outside and stood in the light rain. His beard glistened slightly in the lantern light from the doorway. It was the master.

Ricaldo?

Rose was too heavy-hearted to be careful. Without a word she left the tree and walked towards him. He scowled when she first moved, but his scowl disappeared when he recognized her.

"Go to the end stall near the pump," he whispered.

She stood dully in front of him, and he waved his hand in the right direction.

"Don't let anyone see you."

Rose went through the stable and into the stall. She

didn't try to hide, but the workers were focused on finishing their work. They didn't pay any attention to one more dark figure. The stall was empty, and she sank down in one of its corners. Time passed. She could hear the master yelling at everyone to hurry up. The stable doors slammed shut. Then he was there, standing in the door of the stall, searching the darkness for her.

"You'll have to get your backpack. I won't fit," he said.

"How do you know about my backpack?" Rose was surprised into asking, though she really didn't care. What did it matter?

"Not blind."

Wearily she walked down the aisle and crawled into her hiding place. She pulled the backpack through the tunnel and into the small storage room.

"What happens now?" she asked out loud, though nobody was there to answer her.

The master arrived in a few minutes, pockets bulging.

"I heard Nurse Broomely died," he said, shoving more dried food packages into Rose's backpack. "I'm sorry, child."

Child. That was what Nurse Broomely had called her. Rose's eyes filled again. Where did all the tears come from? She found herself sobbing against this big Yospaldon man as if he were the father she had never known.

He patted her awkwardly on the back.

"She was a fine woman, but she didn't feel good towards the end. She told us that she was ready to go, except for you. We promised we'd take care of you."

"Us!" Rose pulled away, startled again into a little interest. "Who's 'us?'"

"A few of us belong to the Maker here. We help each other and spread the truth when we can."

"Why didn't I know?"

She would have been indignant yesterday or the day before, but she didn't have the strength right now.

"The more people who knew, the more dangerous it was.

We were going to tell you but time got by. We would have soon."

"It doesn't matter," Rose mumbled, and Ricaldo took hold of her shoulders.

"You've got to perk up, child. Nurse Broomely wanted you to escape from this place. Now's the time to do it, and I can help. Look."

He drew a bundle of thin ropes from one of his pockets and showed it to her.

"This is a tree ladder. Ever seen one?"

Rose shook her head.

"The ladder's attached to a long piece of rope weighted at one end. You take the weighted end and throw it over a branch that's too high to reach. It's got to go over and drop down to where you can grab it. It makes a loop, see. Then you pull the loop until the ladder part reaches the branch. You can't climb it yet though, and it won't work tying the two ends together—the loop will travel round the branch every time you stepped on a rung. What you have to do is throw the rope around the branch a couple more times, until the ladder holds tight even with your weight on the rungs. Then you climb it. When you get to the branch, you pull it all up and stow it in your backpack. That's how you can climb a tree that has branches starting way up high. It's safer.

"When you want to get down, you loop the rope around a branch tying one end of the rope securely to the other end. You loop it only once going down. It won't matter if the loop slides around when you're going down unless it slides too fast—hold on to the rope side of the loop to slow it down some. When you reach the ground, you pull the rope around until you can untie it. Then you stow it in your backpack again. Now listen—"

He leaned toward her and fixed Rose's eyes with his own.

"They can't track you with the dogs if you walk in the stream. Travel at night and sleep during the day in a tree above the stream. You've got a hammock in there right?"

Rose nodded. She had two hammocks. *One for me; one for Nurse—*

"Pick a tree with lots of leaf coverage so it will hide you. Never, on any account, leave the stream, not for a single step. You don't want to leave a scent for the dogs to find. Now for it, child. We've got to go. Hop on."

Rose stared perplexed as Ricaldo turned around and bent low.

"I don't understand."

"Frisking fillies," the master said, straightening up and facing her again. "Why doesn't she understand?"

He explained slowly. "Your scent is okay in the stable. Everyone knows you're in here often, but it can't be on the ground heading into the stream. They'll know where you've gone then. I'll boot you over there, but you've got to let me carry you."

Rose hesitated. "If they catch you, they'll—"

Ricaldo snorted. "They'll what? Send me to the Maker? Fine with me. High home's better than this place, I'll warrant. Now hop on."

Rose felt a stirring of warmth within her, but not at the mention of the Maker. She wasn't very happy with the Maker. It was this big, awkward man crouching in front of her who made her feel warm. He was ready to help her, even though it would undoubtedly be the end of his life if he were caught. The feeling gave her the energy to do what Ricaldo wanted. She gave a hop and grabbed hold of his shoulders with her hands. He reached behind and steadied her. Then they were off. It was a lot like riding a very broad horse that walked upright on its hind legs, though a horse couldn't put back an arm to help you stay on. Rose had a sudden desire to laugh loudly. She didn't—but it was a near thing.

They left the stable at its darkest end, went stealthily around the back of the castle, and stopped at a door in the outside wall. Ricaldo pulled a key from a pocket and unlocked the door. Rose wondered dully how he had gotten the key, but she didn't really care. On the other side of the wall, they walked through trees until they reached the bank of a large stream. Ricaldo wouldn't let her get off his back until he'd stumbled down the slight slope of the bank and waded into the water. Then he let her down.

"Follow this stream up the mountain and go down the other side. There are kingdoms better than ours. Find one of them. We'll spread word about you through the Maker's people, and we'll pray for you. Don't give up and don't leave the water!"

He climbed out of the stream and waited on the bank, watching her. It wasn't raining anymore, though the trees above them were still dripping. Rose stood uncertainly in the cold water, looking at him.

"My scent! It's all over your clothes. They'll catch you for sure with the dogs," she said abruptly.

He grinned unexpectedly.

"I've got a tub in my bedroom. It's already got water in it and wood beneath it. I'm going to get that water hot and climb in with my clothes and shoes on. Then I'm going to scrub all over. I did it once when I was two years old, and I've had the urge to do it again ever since."

Rose smiled at him and he smiled back.

"Go on now. The Maker'll take care of you."

Obediently she started walking up the stream, but she sniffed at the idea of the Maker taking care of her.

Three dawns later, Rose managed to throw the rope ladder's weighted end over a branch at the third try—a record! As it fell down the other side of the branch, the end caught on some twigs, but she was able to jerk it free and this time it fell all the way back to the stream. Pulling the ladder up, she tried to throw the weighted rope around the big branch again. The rope caught in a tangle of smaller branches, but it didn't matter. When she tested her weight on the first rung, the ladder held tight. Rose climbed awkwardly, pulled off balance by the pack on her back.

When she reached the big branch, she wanted to sit and rest but made herself pull the ladder up instead. It took a while to untangle the rope from the smaller branches. Eventually she got it free and bunched the ropes together. Stowing them in her pack, she climbed further up the tree until leaves surrounded her. With a sigh, she hooked her hammock on a branch, wrapped up in a blanket, and collapsed in the hammock.

"I wonder how far I've climbed."

For years, Rose had roamed over the hills behind Nurse Broomely's farm. Her legs were strong and she didn't get winded easily. However, walking in a stream was harder than walking on dry land, and traveling at night made it even harder. Sometimes the moon lit her way, but more often than not, big trees overshadowed every step. There were little waterfalls to navigate and big rocks to go around whether she could see them or not. If she could have stepped on some of the smaller rocks, it would have made the climb easier, but then the rocks would have carried her scent.

Her shoes were still on her feet. With a groan, Rose took them off and dropped them in the hammock on top of her blanket. *I wish I had my boots,* but Nurse Broomely's death had filled her mind to the exclusion of practical planning. She still had on the dress and shoes that she'd worn to the court session. Unfortunately the shoes were lightweight. They weren't made for traveling night after night in a stream.

"I've got blisters on top of blisters."

Dawn was over, and early morning sunlight was slowly warming the cold mountain forest. Rose lay in her hammock and thought about food. The meat took so long to chew. *Dried apples, that's what I want.* Suddenly her eyes flew wide open and she grabbed at the edges of her hammock.

Dogs were howling in the distance.

"You knew they would eventually," she told herself and instantly covered her mouth with both hands. No more talking out loud. Sound traveled.

Rose listened for several minutes trying to decide if the dogs were heading in her direction. It was hard to tell. She reached for her backpack and pulled out the first food packet she touched.

"I might as well eat. I won't be able to sleep now," she said and then frowned fiercely.

Stop talking.

As she chewed the dry meat, Rose tried to decide how many dogs were howling. There were definitely more than two or three. Uneasily she pictured the pack of Yospaldon hunting dogs. Their pen was on the other side of the palace from the stable, and she hadn't seen them often, but those few times had been enough. Bred for fierceness as well as tracking abilities, the dogs were big and vicious. Nobody liked them except for their handler, who bragged about them every chance he could get.

"He's proud of how mean they are," Rose said and then sighed in frustration. She'd talked out loud again. Well, it was hard being alone for so long.

Don't talk normal. Keep it low," she told herself in an understanding voice.

After she'd finished the meat, Rose fished around in the backpack for some dried apples to take away her thirst. It was funny: as she trudged up the stream every night with water all around her, she wasn't thirsty, but when she lay in her hammock during the day with no water within reach, she could have drunk glass after glass of fresh water or juice or milk or hot coffee or—

"This is not helping! Maybe an empty food pouch would hold water, if I can get it up the ladder without spilling it," She was speaking in a normal voice again, which was beyond exasperating. *Nervous. I'm so nervous.*

The stream gurgled beneath her and leaves fluttered around her. Despite the distant dog howls, she drifted off to sleep.

When she woke, it was already dark. She'd overslept! Quickly wiggling out of the hammock, Rose stuffed it in her backpack, grabbing the first two food packets that came to hand and sticking them in the top of her dress. She'd eat while she walked. The rope ladder came out last, and she closed the pack, put it on her back, and climbed down to the big branch, where she sat without moving.

"I've got to go," she said and was too uptight to notice she was using a normal voice again.

She continued sitting. "What's the matter?"

Rose shivered. She knew what was the matter. She knew exactly what was the matter. The hunting dogs had howled. They were searching for her. It took several more minutes before she could gather enough courage to fit the rope ladder around the branch and climb down it. Her nerves were definitely on edge that night, and she tried to walk faster but gave it up after a few minutes.

"Nobody can walk fast in water."

It was a frustrating night's walk, but when the morning sun lit the woods around her, she could tell a difference in the trees. They were not only more spread out, they were smaller and scrawny looking. Trees near the top of a mountain were supposed to be small and scrawny. Rose was encouraged until she thought of stopping.

"Where am I going to sleep today?" she asked herself and the words were not only in a normal voice, they trembled.

There weren't any trees high enough or leafy enough to satisfy her, and the higher she got, the scrawnier they became. Finally she climbed a fir tree that leaned over the water. It had plenty of low branches, which meant that she didn't have to use the rope ladder. That was certainly a relief, but the needles were prickly and she couldn't find a very good place to hang her hammock. For the first time, Rose wondered what she was going to do when she got above the timberline.

"I'll, I'll sleep on the ground—or a big rock! I'll climb a big rock."

To distract herself, she nibbled on the dried meat that she was beginning to hate and listened for the dogs. Sure enough, they started howling early in the morning around the same time they'd started yesterday. This time they were closer though.

It was hard to swallow. Silently she put the meat in her hand back into the food pouch. She'd eat it later. Then she lay down and closed her eyes.

"A cave! I'll find a cave. And, and barricade the opening with rocks."

That day Rose rested fitfully. The stream gurgled as it ran over rocks beneath her tree. The gurgle should have been soothing, but it wasn't. For one thing, it made her thirsty, and she had forgotten to carry water up in an empty food pouch. For another, the normally pleasant sound was offset by that day's howling. Several times she woke with a start and listened intently. The dogs seemed to be casting about in different directions. They were always below her on the mountain, but they stayed in her general area.

At last she sat up and dug out a packet of apples to help with her thirst. The sky was growing darker. As soon as those dogs went back to the castle for the night, she'd climb down, but before she started walking, she'd drink her fill. It wouldn't be long. The dogs always—just then a new chorus of howls began and these were closer than any of the others had been. Rose held the sides of her hammock and started crying.

"I can't handle this."

She was exhausted and her feet were in bad shape. The two worst places felt as if they were burning. Rose wasn't a healer, but she had grown up in the country and knew from firsthand experience that burning meant infection. One shoe opened wide at the toes and the other had a gaping hole in the back—it flapped at every step. What was she going to do?

"Help me," she heard herself say.

She hadn't spoken to the Maker since she left Yospaldo. He had let Nurse B die. He/d let the one person who had loved her die, and now Rose was alone. She was sitting on a hammock in a prickly fir tree, and she was alone.

"Nurse Broomely loved you but you deserted her," she hissed, tightening her hands on the hammock until they cramped. "You're not taking care of me either. You're supposed to be good and kind but you're not."

Angry tears ran down her cheeks. For some reason it felt right to tell the Maker exactly what she was feeling. It felt much better than ignoring his existence, but she refused to honor him by lifting her face. She stared at the thick green needles in front of her and clinched her teeth.

Nurse Broomely is with me now.

Rose jumped. If that was true—

She squirmed to a more comfortable position so she could think things through. If it was true that the Maker took his people to a place called the high home after they died ... If that was really true ... Rose dropped her face into her hands.

"We couldn't have escaped together. Nurse B didn't have the strength to travel up a stream or climb a rope ladder, and what else could we have done? There wasn't any other choice."

The girl mulled over that for a while.

"All right, I guess you took care of Nurse Broomely," she admitted grudgingly. "It's me you've abandoned. I'm going to die, you know. If I stay in this tree, I'll die of thirst and if I go down, I'll be killed by those dogs. Or, or something worse."

Rose stopped there. She couldn't name the something worse. It was too scary.

"Do you hear those dogs howling or are you too far

away?"

She didn't have the energy to say anything else. When a dry stick popped nearby, she jumped. Night had come, but the dogs weren't going back to the castle this time. She hadn't left her scent on the ground, but soon they would be close enough to smell her in the tree.

Help me. Please help me.

It was a dark night. Clouds covered the moon and most of the stars. Rose clutched at the prickly fir tree with both hands and waited. Before long, she could hear the dogs running through the underbrush. Their howls were deafening.

Then high, keening on the night breezes, there came a wail. Rose's hands tightened until the fir needles broke her skin, but she didn't notice. Another high wail came, eerie in its swooping call—and another. *So wedewolves are real*, her mind chattered in uncontrollable fright. There was no point in not naming them now. They were coming.

The dogs surged with foolish fury to meet them. They quit howling and started snarling, though that lasted less than a minute. Rose nearly fell out of the tree listening, but all she could hear was a scuffling noise and several yelps that were cut off in the middle.

It was quiet after that.

Chapter 4

WEDEWOLVES

Rose stayed in her fir tree the rest of the night, her heart jumping. When morning came, she climbed stiffly down. She had spent a day and a night in that tree, and she couldn't endure another minute. The gurgle of the stream was driving her crazy.

Kneeling in the stream, the girl scooped water up in her hands until her thirst was satisfied. Then she stood and wiped her mouth and hands on one of the dry parts of her dress.

"Time to move on," she said without making much sound.

It was the first time she had traveled during the day since her escape. She felt uncomfortably exposed by the bright sunlight, but it was the obvious thing to do. The Yospaldons had said that wedewolves hunted at night. If she traveled by day, maybe she could sneak past them.

"No one from the castle will climb this high. I should relax. I'm sure it would be good for me."

Again she spoke very quietly. A whisper would have been louder. Nervousness was still making her talk, but the effort to quit using a normal voice, which had been impossible down in the forested parts of the mountain, was coming easily now. She didn't know if she could have spoken louder if she'd tried. The wedewolves of the high mountain terrain had insisted on proving their existence, and there was nothing she could do about it.

"At least they stopped the Yospaldon hunting dogs. And there's the Maker. He, he'll maybe—"

Her sentence trailed off.

"I hope he'll do something."

She started up the stream again at what felt like a crawling pace. The sun was overhead when the trees ended. Past the timberline, the mountain looked pretty bleak. When summer had fully arrived, the ground would warm up enough to host whatever wild grasses and flowers could survive a high altitude, but at this time of the year there were only rocks and hard earth. Everything was a dull grayish-brown and looked cold. At least she could still walk in the stream, though it was getting smaller.

"I wouldn't want to do without it."

As if the words gave birth to the fact, she went past a big rock and stopped with a gasp. Water was gushing from a hole in front of her. She had climbed to the stream's source.

Rose stared wildly around. The high ground sloped steeply up with patches of snow here and there. Big mounds of snow covered the peak, but she didn't have to go that high. What she needed to do was cross to the other side, but the mountain was very wide at this point. It narrowed considerably as it rose higher though. If she climbed further, the distance to the other side would be less.

She had a short distance left in the stream. Rose splashed forward and then stopped again, staring at the ground above the beginning of the stream. Ever since she had left Yospaldo, the stream had protected her, but from this point on she would leave her scent with every step. Shaking a little and frowning furiously, she lifted her feet out of the water and started walking.

What did you expect? No stream's going to run up one side of the mountain and down the other! Maybe there'll be another stream on the other side. The snow's beginning to melt. There really might be another stream.

Not long after that one of Rose's shoes disintegrated. There was no other word for it. She wasted several precious minutes trying to fix it, but the whole thing fell to pieces in the end. The other shoe was in bad shape too. With sudden decision, she ripped them both off and gingerly held her sore feet, wincing at the touch. A few of the blisters were pretty nasty. She should have brought some medicine. Rose threw the shoes under a rock and went on feeling lightheaded. *It must be the altitude.* Thirty minutes later, she realized that she shouldn't have left the shoes. Something might find them. Something might track her down from them. *It's too late now.*

She was going slower and slower. The soles of her feet felt alternately hot and cold, but the rest of her was consistently cold even though it was the middle of the day. Eventually Rose decided she'd climbed high enough to make the distance around the mountain less. She started going sideways, stopping once to take food from her backpack.

When she looked at her feet, they were swollen. She quit looking at them and kept going. An hour later, a loose rock tripped her and she fell into the shadow of a boulder. It was so much colder in the shade that she gasped. Crawling forward into the sun, she propped her aching feet on a rock. Maybe they'd stop throbbing if she elevated them. Her breathing slowed down as she rested and she didn't feel quite as dizzy.

How am I going to know when I've reached the other side?

Rocks and dirt surrounded her here, exactly as they had when she'd first started going around the mountain. The difference was that the bigger rocks now had long shadows stretching far down the mountain slope. She stared uneasily at them for several minutes before her tired mind realized what they meant.

"The sun's going down. What am I going to do?" she said out loud for the first time since leaving the stream.

Nervousness had made her talk; then it had made her stop talking; now it had made her talk again. The words still didn't make much sound, but what sound there was trembled violently.

Painfully she pulled herself upright again, moaning when her feet touched the ground. *The sun's going down. All right, then I'll go down too. I don't care if it's the best place or not. I've got to get back to the forest.*

It was easier to go down than up. It was even easier to go down than sideways around the mountain. She could breathe better, which meant she wasn't as dizzy—and the tree line was steadily getting closer.

The rock shadows lengthened. A cool breeze picked up and blew across the bare ground. Then the outline of the shadows blurred, and they disappeared. Rose walked faster. The sun had gone behind the mountain; that was all. It wouldn't get dark right away. She had time to reach the trees if she hurried.

Even with the exercise, her teeth were chattering. She wished she had brought a jacket. There was her blanket, but she didn't want to stop and unpack.

When a dark object loomed up on her right, Rose instinctively shied away from it.

"A tree! It's a tree!"

She'd been concentrating on where to step for so long that she'd forgotten to check on the tree line. A few stunted firs were already on either side of her.

"Not long now. Reach the forest. I'll be safe in the forest."

She couldn't think clearly, but the forest meant safety. The wedewolves wouldn't find her in the forest. They didn't hunt there. Did they?

Can't think.

It was definitely getting dark now, but she was passing more and more trees. In a few more steps—then the eerie, drawn-out wail of a wedewolf drifted through the air.

"No," she whimpered and started to run despite the pain in her feet.

She was in the forest at last but would the trees really

protect her? Her mind chose that moment to remember the Yospaldon hunting dogs. Wedewolves had come into the forest to attack them. They wouldn't hesitate to follow a lone girl, easy prey. Another and another wail sliced through the air. They were on her trail. They had to be. Rose ran through the forest, no longer trying to find the best place to put her hurt feet. She had forgotten about climbing a tree. She ran like a hunted animal fleeing in panic from stronger, faster foes. The wails rose in evil harmony, steadily gaining on her.

A mass of tall mountain bushes appeared in front of her. Closely intertwined branches were everywhere except for one place at ground level.

It might have been the way the branches grew; it might end in three feet, but it looked like a path and Rose plunged straight into it. The forest had been dark but thick leaves surrounded her now, blocking what little light the night sky provided. Rushing blindly onwards, she guided herself with her hands. It was a wonder she didn't fall, but a low light had come into view up ahead, and that steadied her.

The light marked the end of the path. Racing out of the mass of bushes, Rose found herself at the top of a hillock that stood above a small clearing. There wasn't time to take it all in. One hurried step further was as far as she got before a foot caught on an exposed root and she rolled down the slope. Something soft stopped her. She lay without moving, eyes closed tight. Unfortunately, closing her eyes didn't make everything go away. The howls of the wedewolves came closer; the something soft stayed soft and solid against her back.

Then it shifted and her eyes sprang open. She found herself staring at the head of a mountain sheep. There were two of them—the one that had kept her from rolling any further and the one next to it. The two sheep were lying on the grass, chewing as if they were settling down for a peaceful night's sleep. Their expressions were placid and calm, which was remarkable considering the fiendish wails that had taken over that part of the mountain world.

A movement at the top of the slope made Rose tense convulsively. The clearing was lit by the night sky, but it was dark where the bushes ended, so dark that she could barely see the tall stag with massive antlers that stood facing the small party of three at the bottom of the slope.

The stag turned. Its antlers swept across the night sky. Then it was gone.

In less than a minute, the wails veered sharply off to the right. At the same time they increased in intensity, as if the wedewolves had sighted prey that interested them more than a girl who couldn't run fast. *The stag!*

Rose listened, hardly daring to believe what her ears were telling her. Maybe the hunters would change their minds and come back—but they didn't. Their wails were harder to hear as they got further away. Then they abruptly cut off. The wedewolves must have gone around the mountain.

"I hope they don't catch that stag," she said with a catch in her throat.

If she had met the tall animal with its huge antlers alone in the forest, she would have been terrified, but it seemed, it really did seem as if it had deliberately led the wedewolves away.

Don't let them hurt it, she found herself begging.

Of course, whether the wedewolves caught up with the stag or not, they might get back on her trail. They never quit, the Yospaldons said. What should she do?

The sheep continued slowly chewing, and Rose found herself yawning. It had been the most horrible day of her life; her body was freezing; her feet were throbbing; her nerves were out-of-control. Nevertheless she yawned and looked once more at the sheep. Their thick horns curled back in circles. Large bodies of wool bunched out behind their faces. At a different time, she might have laughed at the big bodies, small heads, and jaws that went on steadily, reassuringly chewing. Rose yawned again and curled up close to the sheep that had stopped her fall.

The second sheep pushed to its feet and ambled to her other side. With a contented grunt, it settled down almost on top of her. Thick, luxurious wool was on either side and above her. Rose felt its soft insistent warmth for less than a minute before falling into a deep sleep.

A fire crackled nearby. It was a pleasant sound. Rose lay drowsily and listened to it until an air current moved a hair on her neck, tickling her. Without opening her eyes, she began to lift a hand to push away the hair, but the hand dropped down again. Her arm was sore.

It was tempting to sink back into sleep, but she made herself open her eyes. The darkness that met her gaze was what she expected to see. It had been nighttime after all when she'd gone to sleep, but the rough wooden beams over her head weren't supposed to be there.

Still partially asleep, Rose puzzled over them. The fire crackled once more and she turned her head toward it. A half-circle of firelight illuminated a rough wooden floor. She couldn't see much else when she looked around, but Rose could tell by the very feel of things that she was in a small room, though she couldn't remember how she had gotten there. The cot under her wasn't very comfortable, but there were warm blankets over her.

She had to change positions. One leg was bent at the knee while the other was straight. From the feel of things, they had been in that position for a long time. She had to move them. With an effort, she straightened one leg and bent the other.

The new position was a relief, but the blankets rubbed gently across her feet as she moved them, and Rose had to bite her lips to keep from crying out. Something stirred on the other side of the room. Then there were footsteps, coming toward her. Rose shrank into the cot, but that didn't stop the dark form of a man from leaning over her.

He placed a hand on her forehead. "Are you awake? Your temperature's—"

Rose clenched her fists and hit at his chest. Fear gave strength to her arms. The man stumbled backwards and sat down hard on the floor next to the cot.

"What was that—" he began asking indignantly, but Rose interrupted him.

"Don't touch me!"

"I—"

"Leave me alone, do you hear!"

The man sat as if thinking it over. When he got to his feet, Rose shrank as far from him as she could on the narrow cot, but he didn't step in her direction. Instead he put more wood on the fire and returned to the other side of the room.

Moving her legs had hurt. In fact, now that she was completely awake, Rose could tell that every part of her body hurt. The night slowly passed. She had time to decide that her legs hurt the most, with the exception of her feet, which were in a category all by themselves. As the hours passed, each foot throbbed worse and worse until she had to bite her lips again to keep from moaning.

Dawn brought a dim light into the room. Rose looked frantically around; she was in a small, dirty, one-room cabin. The man was sleeping on the floor across from her.

He's a young man. That's bad. I've got to get out of here.

With a tremendous effort, she pushed herself up. She did it very quietly, but the young man instantly stirred and sat up too. He rubbed a hand across his eyes and yawned. Then he glanced at her.

"I'm leaving," Rose hissed like a cat and felt like one too—a very angry cat with fur bristling on its back, claws outstretched and ready.

"Are you now? Don't you want more salve on your feet first?" he responded in an unexpectedly pleasant manner.

"No," she said.

Is there a salve that will help my feet?
Rose wanted it.
Give me the salve; you go away.

She swung her legs over the side of the bed and her feet touched the floor. In an instant they were back on the bed and she was leaning over them, clenching her teeth.

What am I going to do?

The man was there then, dipping his hand into a small container.

"The touch will hurt at first, but the salve will numb your feet. It will help for a couple of hours."

He bent down and touched the bottom of a foot. Rose screamed and thrashed about, but the man held her feet one at a time and applied the salve quickly. He was right about its effects. The numbing came immediately, and Rose felt relief so intense that she couldn't speak.

"Right—I'll get water and we'll have breakfast."

He walked to a filthy little window in the front of the cabin and peered out. When he stayed there, Rose lifted her head and stared at him. He wasn't particularly tall and his sandy-colored hair was closely cut around his head as if he didn't want to bother with it. The Yospaldon women wouldn't have liked either of those things. They liked tall men with long hair that they could curl around their fingers. They would have liked this man's face and build though. They would have liked the color of his hair and his alert brown eyes. *Bleh.* Her eyes narrowed. She could clearly hear water running outside. There must be a river or a stream next to the cabin. Why wasn't the man getting water like he'd said?

"Afraid to get wet?"

"What?" the man asked, turning away from the window.

"You were going for water."

He turned back to the window.

"Yes, I was, but I don't think I will after all. I don't like the company I'd have if I left the cabin."

Rose froze. She didn't know how she had gotten to that

cabin. She couldn't remember anything that happened after she fell asleep between the two mountain sheep, but she remembered quite clearly what had happened before then.

"What's there?" she asked shakily.

"Wedewolves," the man answered matter-of-factly.

Rose's eyes darted about in a panic, but the walls of the small cabin were solid. She was safe enough if you counted being alone with a strange man safe. Then her eyes focused on the light seeping in through the dirty window, and she corrected the man sharply.

"They can't be. Wedewolves don't hunt during the day. Everybody knows that."

The man didn't answer. He continued standing by the window, staring outside. Several minutes passed.

"Did you actually see a wedewolf?" Rose asked as insultingly as possible. She didn't trust this man. She'd almost rather be at the mercy of a wedewolf.

He didn't answer her question. The cabin's back corner had captured his attention, the one on the other side of the fire from Rose's cot. Swiftly he moved to the fire and drew out a thick stick of wood burning brightly on one end. He went to the corner he had been staring at and pushed the red-hot end of the stick against the side wall, a foot from the corner and four inches up from the floor. A sliver of wood from the burning stick fell to the floor, but he didn't seem concerned. He stepped on it with his heavy boots and kept on holding the stick to the wall. Smoke began to fill the room.

Rose gazed wildly around again. She was trapped in a dirty cabin by a lunatic and she couldn't stand up, much less walk. Lying back on her pillow, the girl closed her eyes. She needed to decide what to do. It was absolutely urgent to decide what to do. Unfortunately, nothing came to mind.

The minutes passed slowly. Then smoke wafted over to her side of the cabin and made her cough. That did it. She couldn't stay quiet any longer. It might be hopeless, but someone had to try and talk this man out of burning the cabin down with them in it. She would use easy words that would get through to him.

"Are you crazy?" burst from her mouth. It wasn't exactly what she'd meant to say, though it did seem to fit the occasion.

"No," the man answered, not even glancing in her direction.

He threw the stick into the fire. Then he picked up another one and moved quickly over to the place on the wall that was now smoldering. A billow of thick smoke crept along the floor.

"Yes, you are. Why else would you want to burn the wall?"

He laughed.

"I told you already what I was going to do."

He started to say more, but his laughter had infuriated Rose. The Yospaldons had laughed at her too.

"You said you were getting water. Why don't you?" she spat out, leaning forward.

He laughed again as he carefully applied the burning end of the stick to the wall.

"I am," he answered her evenly.

The fact that he was the one staying calm and not her infuriated Rose even more than his laughter. "You're insane," she sputtered.

"It's not the usual method, I'll admit, but since I don't care to be eaten by wedewolves, I'll take it. Breakfast will be later than I planned. My cereal needs hot water to soften it. Do you think you can wait or do you want some of the dried food from your backpack?"

"You went through my things," Rose protested with fresh outrage.

"Of course I did, for several reasons."

"You had no right. Stay out of my backpack from now on," she ordered in the snooty manner she'd once heard a Yospaldon countess use. She had despised the countess at the time but didn't mind copying her now if it would keep this man away from her.

He didn't answer. The wall wasn't in flames but there was the beginning of a hole in its side now. The man threw the stick into the fire and pulled a knife from his belt. He scraped a large clump of fire-blackened wood out of the hole with the knife and then went to the fire for another stick with a red-hot end. Rose watched through narrowed eyes. She didn't want to talk to this man; she didn't want anything to do with him, but as the silence grew, she couldn't help bringing something back up.

"Did you actually see a wedewolf?" she asked and couldn't keep a tremor out of her words.

He answered gently, "More than one. Daytime isn't their preferred time to hunt, but they will follow a quarry until they catch it or die in the attempt. It's not that they're hungry."

There was an edge to his voice, as if he were upset about something. Rose put it down to cowardice and gave herself another reason to despise him. Five minutes later, a swirl of thick smoke moved over the cabin floor straight up her nose. She coughed heavily and one of her feet bumped against the blanket, bringing tears to her eyes. The numbing effect of the salve must be wearing off. She clenched her teeth.

I'd rather die than ask him for more.

Ten more minutes went by with the man boring deeper and deeper into the wall. Rose lay motionless on her cot, bracing herself against the pain that grew until both feet were throbbing once more. Eventually the man stopped and examined his hole. Then he walked to the front of the cabin where he studied a crack in the floor as if it were of utmost interest. Rose couldn't stand it.

"How many holes does your cabin have? Not enough obviously, since you spent all morning making another one. Maybe you could sweep a little of the dirt into that crack you're so interested in."

She stared disdainfully around the dirty room.

"It's not my cabin," the man muttered in Rose's direction,

but he wasn't really paying attention to her.

Instead he reached for his knife again and started widening the crack where it was slightly rotten at the edges. The wood yielded quickly to his sharp blade. Before long he had made a sizeable hole.

Rose heard something leap onto the porch outside and gasped with renewed fear. This lunatic was going to let the wedewolves inside the cabin. All they had to do was go under the porch—but the man ran quickly back to the hole he had made in the back wall and stabbed the center of it with his knife.

Water gushed from it, a swiftly moving stream that flowed straight across the cabin floor and out the widened crack as if it had been told what to do.

Chapter 5

BENK

The man watched the stream running through the cabin. Possibly he was making sure his plan had no glitches in it, though he didn't look worried.

Rose made up for that. She swallowed convulsively and watched the stream too. It was a foot wide and about two inches deep on the flat floor. *The rush of the current must keep it from spreading all over the floor.*

About the same time she came up with this important observation, the man nodded in a satisfied way and hung a pot filled with water on a nail over the fire. Then he jumped across the stream, picked up his blanket and pack, and jumped back. There wasn't enough room for him to stretch out on the far side of the cabin now. He would have to sleep on Rose's side. A corner of Rose's mind told her she should object loudly, but she was still staring wide-eyed at the powerful flow of water running across the floor of the cabin.

"Breakfast in twenty minutes," the man said a bit smugly.

"The wedewolves—"

"They won't enter water moving that fast."

"If it spreads—"

"I don't think it will."

"That's not reassuring," she informed him. He laughed in response, and Rose jerked forward. "Don't laugh at me," she growled.

The young man's head turned in surprise. He studied her for a minute while she stared defiantly back. The throbbing in her feet was making the calves of her legs hurt now.

"You're in pain again. I'm sorry. It's sooner than I expected."

He sounded kind. Rose's eyes narrowed as he went for the salve. She couldn't let herself trust him. There was no man alive who could be trusted—unexpectedly a name slipped into her mind.

"Ricaldo!" she blurted out loud.

Along with the name had come a vivid mental picture of the bearded man smiling on the edge of a stream. He had carried her into it.

"What did you say?" the young man asked, straightening from his pack with the small container of salve in his hand.

"Nothing," Rose said and braced for the pain.

It wasn't quite as bad as last time, but it was bad enough. She didn't scream again, but by the time he had spread the potent cream over her second foot, she was covered with sweat. Fortunately the blessed numbness was already at work.

The man put the container back in his pack and busied himself with something. Rose didn't care what he was doing. All she'd done that morning was lie in bed, but she was exhausted. When he suddenly appeared at her side, she tensed automatically, but her body didn't have the energy to do anything else.

"I've got your breakfast," he explained and started to help her sit up.

"I can take care of myself," she snapped, which was so obviously untrue that she blushed.

He stood silently holding the bowl of hot cereal as she maneuvered herself to a sitting position. The smell of toasted oats and honey filled the air, and she reached eagerly for the bowl as soon as she could. The man gave it to her and retreated to the floor by his pack.

"Let me explain who I am."

"About time," Rose found time to say in-between bites. *Um-m-m*. There were raisins too! The warm nourishing food felt good both in her mouth and in her empty stomach.

"I am a scout for the Kingdom of Far Reaches. Most people have heard of us."

He paused expectantly, but when Rose just scowled at him, he shrugged and continued.

"We're a small kingdom many miles southwest of here. I was sent to explore the area and see what kingdoms might be located in this part of Montaland. My name is Benk."

He paused again as if she might recognize the name.

"Never heard of you," Rose told him.

His jaw set, but he responded evenly.

"There was word sent to a Yospaldon I know. A fourteen-year-old girl was traveling over the mountain."

Rose jumped before she could stop herself. Ricaldo had said he would spread the word to others like himself, others who trusted the Maker.

Benk nodded. *I thought so.*

"My informant told me that she was in need of help," was all he said to the girl though.

"Who was your informant?" she asked.

It was Benk's turn to narrow his eyes.

"I can't tell you. If he was found out, he'd be killed."

The girl chewed busily as she mulled that over. She seemed to accept it because her next question changed the subject. "How did you find me?"

Benk didn't mind answering this time.

"I heard the wedewolf pack howling last night and knew they were after someone. It wasn't until the sun rose though that we found you."

He didn't add that he'd been puzzled by the dryness of the grass right around her. The small clearing had been completely shadowed in the early morning by tall forest trees. Most of the grass had been covered with thick dew, except for what was near the girl, and she had been as dry and warm as if she'd slept under a thick comforter all night. Even her hands and ears, the first places to get cold, had been comfortably warm.

"How did you escape the wedewolves?" he asked, not really expecting her to tell him. To his surprise, she answered.

"There was a stag. He led them away. I don't know if they caught him or not."

Her eyes were fixed on something that wasn't in this cabin, and he knew she'd forgotten he was there. Her face scrunched up in an effort to control her tears, though a few ran down her cheeks anyway.

Benk whistled.

"One of the Maker's stags! I've heard of them but never met anyone who's seen one. I don't think you have to worry about wedewolves catching him—not a stag from the high home. What was he like?"

"It was dark and I couldn't see very well," she said, caught up in the memory. "He was tall, I know. His antlers were huge. They swept the sky when he moved."

She seemed to remember where she was then and lifted her chin, sniffing back her tears. Benk watched her. Maybe she'd keep on talking.

"It was a cold night and there was dew on the grass, but your body was dry and warm when we found you." She considered him haughtily.

"That would be the sheep, I expect," she said, lifting her nose and sniffing.

"The sheep," he repeated, rubbing his chin.

Rose could tell he didn't believe her. He was acting as if she were the crazy one, not him, so she condescended to explain.

"Yes, the Maker sent two of his sheep to keep me warm.

They lay on either side of me."

She tried to keep the lofty tone of one accustomed to such things happening, but the memory of those dear sheep made her want to cry again. She wished they were on either side of her now, not because she needed their warmth, but for the sheer comfort of their presence.

Benk whistled again, which was gratifying. There was less chance of him attacking her if he considered her important. He was only indirectly from Ricaldo. She really didn't know whether she could trust him or not. He talked as if he knew the Maker, but that didn't raise him very much in Rose's opinion, because she was still not sure about the Maker. He had come through with those sheep though—and the stag! It was confusing.

Something thumped on the cabin porch. Benk was at the small window before Rose could blink. He stared through it for several minutes while she twisted the blanket tightly between her fingers, waiting for him to tell her what was going on. However, when he left the window, he didn't say anything.

Rose had to know. Her fingers were beginning to hurt, and the blanket might never be the same again.

"What is it?"

"Huh. Oh, the wedewolves," he answered, an expression of pain on his face.

"They'll never leave. They'll wait us out," Rose whispered, twisting the blanket tighter. "What are you going to do?"

She asked the question as rudely as she could, but the strange thing was that she expected an answer. This scout had managed to get water for them. What would he do next?

Benk turned toward her, and she tensed under his steady gaze.

"We'll leave in the boat, but we'll have to wait a couple of weeks. The river's not high enough now."

"You aren't making any sense," Rose told him as if he were a four-year-old.

"Until then, we're not badly off. We have plenty of wood and food, and now there's water for drinking and bathing."

In an instant Rose was quivering with indignation. "I am not going to bathe in this cabin while you're here!"

Benk shook his head. "I'll let you know when I wash and you look the other way. When you wash, I'll heat water in the kettle and bring it to you. I don't mind standing at the window for however long it takes you."

Rose's fingers let go of their death grip on the blanket. *Ah ha. I don't smell good, do I?* She hadn't bothered to bathe when she was struggling up the mountain in the stream. Then there had been the trek over the high part of the mountain, crowned off by her panicked run from the wedewolves. She patted her bulging middle piece, firmly secured in place. It had been saturated with sweat upon sweat. Probably the stink in it wouldn't wash out if she tried—but she didn't plan to try.

Over the next week and a half Rose consistently refused to wash. She noticed that Benk held his breath whenever he brought her food. He chose to sit in the far corner of the cabin. A number of long branches with green leaves on them were stacked in that corner. He seemed to enjoy stripping the leaves off and trimming the branches down to a sharp point. It finally dawned on Rose what he was doing.

"You're making arrows, aren't you?"

"Yeah, I didn't have many left. I gathered the green wood on the way to the cabin."

"Why are you making so many?"

"I've been counting the wedewolves. There are twelve of them, so I'll need twelve arrows," Benk answered cheerfully.

Rose laughed. She was getting along a little better with the young man. The knowledge of her potent aroma relaxed her.

"I'd make a few more—in case you miss once or twice,"

she said almost pleasantly.

Benk grinned and cut a notch in the end of the arrow he was working on.

"Are you going to tell me your name?" he asked nonchalantly.

"No."

Every day he asked what to call her, and Rose refused each time to tell him. She was more relaxed; she might even admit that she enjoyed Benk's company, but telling him her name wasn't something she could bring herself to do. It would make them friends if he said her name in his kind way. She couldn't accept that.

Outside, the sky started darkening into night.

The light was dimming in his corner. Picking up the last two unstripped branches, Benk went closer to the fire. He was halfway through stripping leaves off one of them when a sudden snarling announced the arrival of their unwanted visitors. Two or three of the wedewolves had jumped onto the porch and were quarreling over who got to be nearest to the window. Since no one ever came out of the door, they'd given up on it and concentrated their attention on the window.

They knew whenever Benk walked near it. He never heard any snarling then. The wedewolves got very quiet, but it was the quiet of focused hostility.

"I'm glad that window is small," the girl said in a trembling voice.

Her voice always trembled when she was thinking of the wedewolves. Benk glanced at her. The last few nights he had moved over to the fire when it got dark. He needed its light to work on his arrows, but the change in place had put him close to her cot. The interesting thing was that she hadn't complained. He didn't think she had even noticed. Without realizing it, she was growing to trust him.

He spoke to her reassuringly.

"We'll get out of here soon, and you can wave goodbye to the wedewolves. How are your feet?" he ended in an abrupt change of subject.

She slowly wiggled her toes.

"They're not quite as swollen, but the cuts don't look good and two of the bruises have developed giant yellow places."

"It's good the bruises are yellow. They become yellow as they heal," Benk told her.

"I don't think I can walk on them yet," she admitted, her forehead wrinkling with worry.

"You won't have to walk. The boat will carry you," he reminded her patiently.

Rose lay on her bed and fretted, but she didn't ask any more questions. She wanted to believe Benk had a plan. She wanted to believe it very badly, though she couldn't imagine what it was. Even if he carried her to the boat—and her nose rose an inch at the very idea—how would they ever reach it with wedewolves on the porch?

The next morning she woke early and lifted herself on one elbow, listening. Up to now the river outside the cabin had made the pleasant sound of water splashing over rocks. Their indoor stream had flowed through the cabin with a powerful but cheerful swishing noise. Something had changed overnight though. The stream was hurtling along the cabin floor as if it were angry. Outside, the river wasn't splashing pleasantly any longer. It was roaring as if it had doubled in size.

"The river's louder."

Benk snored slightly in his corner.

"The river's louder!" Rose repeated, getting a good bit louder herself.

With a start the scout jumped to his feet, hurried to the

window, and looked intently through the dirty glass. Then he turned to his backpack and grabbed two things from it, his knife and what seemed at first glance a child's bow. Rose studied the bow with interest. It was small but quite a bit thicker than normal.

A child couldn't bend that bow. I guess it's small so it will fit inside a backpack.

Benk walked over to the window, lifted his knife, and deliberately broke the glass.

Rose gasped.

"The wedewolves," she spluttered.

Benk didn't answer. A dun-colored snout appeared in the broken part of the glass. Its mouth snarled at them, baring dirty-white fangs, and Rose screamed. Benk waited, knife in hand. He was ready for action but didn't seem surprised. Rose, who had stopped screaming because you can't scream when you aren't breathing, stared at him and the wedewolf. There was a moment of silence.

With a sudden lunge, the wedewolf pushed out the rest of the glass. The logs around the window were not so easily moved. They didn't budge. Only the narrow head could get through the opening. Rose could see the orange eyes glaring at them, and for some reason her mind darted back to the conversation of the young Yospaldon men at the Welcome to Spring Reception. They had been talking about wedewolves and she'd stopped to gather information. Now she knew more than they did.

Wedewolves do have pupils in their eyes, black ones. Furthermore, it's not their howls that immobilize prey; it's the evil in their eyes, she told the young men in her mind, absurdly glad to be proving them wrong.

This interesting conversation lasted ten seconds. That was how long it took Rose's body to breath and promptly scream again.

At the same moment Benk struck with his knife, plunging it into the side of the wedewolf's head and instantly drawing it out again. Orange eyes closed as the mouth opened to howl, but the howl never came. For a moment the body of the dead wedewolf was held by the tight fit of its head within the window. Then the head slithered out of sight onto the porch.

Dropping his knife, Benk grabbed up his bow and an arrow. He sprang to the window and sighted, drawing the thick bow to an unbelievable curve before releasing it. The arrow flew through the window and Rose heard a wedewolf start to howl then stop. Benk had another arrow on string and bow bent in no time, but he didn't shoot it.

"They've gone for now," he said over his shoulder.

Dropping the arrow he had, the scout reached behind his backpack and picked up another one. He fitted it into his bow and sighted along it, but something was wrong with the new arrow. It had a long piece of string tied to it. Rose would have shouted a warning if she'd had any words left, but the events of the last few minutes had left her speechless.

He bent the bow almost double this time. When the arrow shot out the window, Rose strained her ears to hear a cut-off howl, but there wasn't one this time. Had he missed?

Benk picked up another arrow with a string attached and shot it also through the window. Rose sat as high as she could and craned her neck. Hidden from sight by the scout's big backpack and conveniently next to the window was a small pile of arrows with brown strings tied to them, only now that she looked at them more closely, the strings looked more like twine.

One by one Benk shot the small pile of arrows. Then he reached into his backpack for a larger arrow. This one had a metal tip, so he couldn't have made it in the cabin. He must have been saving it. Very carefully he aimed and shot. As soon as he'd released that arrow, he dropped his bow and grabbed up a length of wood that was positively fuzzy with the ends of all the twine. Quickly he turned the wood and as it turned, the twine started winding around it.

Rose stared. She didn't understand what he was trying to do, but she muttered anyway, "Help him, Maker, please help him."

Something bumped the porch. There was a scraping sound. Benk gave the length of wood a final turn and tossed it out the window. Immediately he sped to the door of the cabin and threw it wide open. Rose opened her mouth, but she was so shocked, nothing came out. The scout ran onto the porch and then darted inside again, dragging a small boat with him. The boat's side was stuck full of arrows with brown twine attached to them.

After the boat cleared the threshold, Benk sprang for the door and slammed it shut. It was none too soon. Something jumped onto the porch; then something else, and the wedewolves snarled with fury over the escape of their prey. Benk grabbed his bow and an arrow and ran to the window, but the wedewolves were too smart to be caught that way again. They were out of sight already but not too far away. Rose could hear their snarling frustration.

Benk faced her.

"Our boat," he announced with a flourish.

"I thought it was tied," she managed to say.

"It was. I had to cut the rope with a metal-tipped arrow. After the rope was cut, I could pull the boat toward the cabin with the twine."

Rose stared at him and he explained further.

"Twine's stronger than string. One length wouldn't have been enough, but several worked pretty well. It's a good thing the boat was old and its wood could be penetrated by the wooden arrow tips. I didn't have enough metal ones."

He stopped talking, obviously satisfied with the success of his plan.

Rose transferred her stare to the boat. The twine looped down its side but only a little. The wood piece with the twine ends wrapped around it lay neatly in the bottom of the boat where Benk had tossed it. He had saved boat, arrows, and twine.

"You're crazy!" Rose said; however, she didn't say it with the scorn she would have used a week ago. The scout reached for the pot and filled it with water.

"Breakfast coming up."

By the time the water had heated and the cereal had softened, Rose had recovered enough to talk.

"I want to know what you're planning next, Benk."

She stopped short at the look of pleasure that spread over the young man's face. It was the first time she had called him by his name. Her face got hot when she realized what she'd done, but Benk just responded conversationally to what she had said.

"I'm not sure that's a good idea. You'll think it's crazy."

"Is it?"

Pouring her share of the cereal into the wooden bowl from his pack, he handed the bowl to her, along with the spoon. He would make do with his cup as usual, slurping the thick cereal down slowly.

"A little," he admitted, staring at the cup. "I should have whittled another spoon."

Rose would not be sidetracked.

"I don't want another surprise like the one you gave me this morning. It was awful not to know what was happening. We have the boat in the cabin now, but how can we get on the river? There are obstacles in the way, obstacles with teeth."

Benk leaned against the wall. An expression of amusement came over his face. He was enjoying this!

If he laughs at me—

Quickly Rose put a big bite of cereal into her mouth. She didn't want to snap at him right now. It would interrupt his explanation.

"The river's rising," he said and waited for her to confirm that fact.

"Um hmm," was all she could manage without spraying cereal all over the cabin.

"When I found this cabin, I noticed water marks on both of the side walls, so I did some figuring. The river flows down the mountain several feet to the right of the cabin most of the year. In the spring though, snow from high on the mountain melts into the river, making it overflow its banks. First it runs up against the cabin's right side. That's how I was able to get our drinking water. Later the river will rise even higher. Then it will run on both sides of the cabin."

"What's to stop the flooding river from sweeping the cabin off with us in it?" Rose asked.

"The builder of the cabin thought of that," Benk said with such an air of smugness that Rose had to take another big bite.

"You weren't awake to see it when we brought you here, but there's a large boulder behind the cabin. I think it divides the fully flooding river into two. One half goes right; the other, left. The two halves come together again beyond the porch. Now that we've got the boat inside, we can leave whenever the river rises high enough. We'll push the boat off the porch and leisurely hop in it. The wedewolves can howl all they want to—we'll be away from here."

Rose had another question. "What if there are wedewolves on the porch?"

"They won't be. They know I'll shoot them there."

"Smug" doesn't do him justice. Neither does "self-satisfied." There's another word that's better, but I can't remember what it is.

She scraped her bowl and popped what was left into her mouth.

After he'd explained his plan, Benk seemed to be waiting. He was probably wondering what objections she'd make next. Rose swallowed her last bite—and smiled. She surprised herself as much as she did the young man in front of her, who looked stunned.

"How many arrows do you have left?" she asked.

"I'll have to pull out the ones I shot into the boat and see what shape they're in, but I should have plenty."

"Make sure you have ten," she said and put her bowl down. "I'm done."

Benk grinned.

"Two wedewolves down, ten to go, huh?"

She rolled her eyes.

"Come to think of it, you should make extra. Thirty, maybe forty."

Chapter 6

THE RIVER RISES

The river rose steadily that day, making conversation impossible by afternoon. Rose dreaded the approach of night. She woke with a start several times during the night. It sounded as if a giant on the right side of the cabin was bellowing at a smaller giant on the left side of the cabin, on and on and on. By the time she woke the next morning, the giant on the left was bellowing back.

She ate her hot cereal, but all she could do after that was listen nervously to the thunderous roar and watch Benk. The paddle to the boat was old and thin. The scout was strapping strips of wood onto the weakest places. Rose hoped he knew what he was doing. The new confidence she had gained in him was not lasting very well against a backdrop of two giants roaring at each other.

It was almost noon when something cracked loudly.

Rose didn't know what it was, but Benk stiffened where he sat. Then he sprang to his feet and threw the reinforced paddle into the boat. Spinning around, he seized his pack. It was in the air heading for the middle of the boat when the arrows he had piled beside the boat followed it. Next he charged at Rose, who was still confused and didn't know whether to fight him or not. He grabbed her while she was trying to decide and put her into the front seat of the boat.

"What are you doing?" Rose shouted.

"Stay there," he ordered as he raced for her pack and the blankets she'd been using.

Whipping the blankets around her pack, he threw them both into the boat and was snatching the pot from its hook when another loud crack came.

Rose clutched at the sides of the boat. Now she understood. The wall on the right was breaking away from the rest of the cabin. The furious stream of water rushing through its hole, combined with the river pounding on its outside, was proving to be too much for the old logs.

There is very little in nature more powerful than a mighty surge of water. On the heels of the second crack came a third, and the wall began to break apart.

"Benk!" screamed Rose.

Water poured through the cracks, lifting the little boat and turning it sideways. Rose grabbed the paddle and tried to make the boat go toward Benk without much success. It was like a leaf trying to battle its way upstream. Fortunately the cabin wasn't very big. Benk pushed through the fierce current that rose above his knees even while Rose watched. When he reached the boat, he threw the pot in, grabbed the side of the boat so he could make it face forward again, and jumped for the back of the boat. He landed on the seat right as the front wall of the cabin collapsed.

With a huge burst of energy, the river propelled them out of the dark cabin into brilliant noon sunshine. There was a crash behind them and Rose twisted around to see the cabin's roof gone. The fire in the fireplace was still tranquilly burning in the back wall. Then the other side wall fell. She didn't see what happened to the fire.

Benk was shouting at her, "The paddle, give me the paddle."

Hastily she shoved the paddle she was holding at him. They were racing down the river gloriously fast, but they were too close to the bank. Something else was racing down the bank parallel to the river and uncomfortably close to them, but even as Rose shrank from the wedewolves, Benk guided the boat into the middle of the river. It wasn't an extremely wide river, but it was wide enough to put a safe distance between them and the wedewolves.

Suddenly Rose felt exhilarated. It was wonderful to be out of that musty old cabin into warm sunshine with fresh air whipping through her hair. Benk must have felt it too. He whooped and she turned so she could smile at him.

"Isn't this great?" he yelled.

"Yes! But weren't we supposed to hop leisurely into the boat? What happened to your plan?"

"Changed it," Benk said. He shrugged his shoulders and winked at her.

No man had ever winked at Rose without receiving an ugly scowl back. She didn't know what to do. Everything was so happy. She faced forward once again. Then she scowled, but since Benk was behind her, it didn't have much effect. *Oh well.*

The river carried them away from the mountain and through a long winding valley. Once a large pile of brush behind them that must have been lighter than their boat came winging down the current. It threatened to crash into them, but Benk was on the lookout for that sort of thing and expertly maneuvered them out of the way. He also watched for heavy logs in front of them that wouldn't be going as fast as their boat. These were sometimes under the surface of the water with only a twig or two poking up. If their boat crashed into a submerged log, it could be disastrous.

Rose helped him steer clear of the hidden logs since she was in the front of the boat. Usually Benk saw them first, but she soon learned what to look for and once called a warning before he spotted anything.

"Good job!" he praised her and she could feel her face glow. When was the last time she'd gotten a compliment?

The wedewolves ran on the river bank beside them for

the first hour. They had to go flat out at first, but as the river widened, the current slowed and all they had to do was lope along easily. Rose was elated when they disappeared from sight.

"We've left them behind," she said over her shoulder.

"Maybe," Benk replied cryptically.

Rose didn't want to hear that. She deliberately didn't ask what he meant. Of course they had left the wedewolves behind. They weren't there anymore, were they?

When Benk asked her to find his bow and arrows, she was glad to have something to do even though it meant she had to turn around in a narrow space. Sure enough, her feet banged against the side of the boat, making her wince with pain, but she found the bow and arrows without any problem and shoved them triumphantly towards Benk. The scout took them without comment; he was staring at the river ahead with narrowed eyes. Her heart sank. *What now?*

Whatever it was, Rose didn't want to meet it sitting backwards in the boat. She swung her legs over the seat again, managing not to hit her feet this time, and faced forwards. There wasn't anything she could see to worry about—nothing to warrant the scout's hard stare.

The river had been making a wide curve for several minutes to avoid a range of mountains that rose steeply on its right bank. Left of them was a long stretch of grassland. Low mountains sloped up the other side of the grasslands. It was the kind of place that might make good farmland someday. The river curved further left, bringing a stand of trees into view.

Rose inhaled sharply. There were wedewolves standing among that stand of trees, ten wedewolves, waiting for them. A high-pitched wail keened through the air.

"How did they get in front of us?" she asked in dismay.

"Cut off a loop of the river by heading straight over those low mountains," Benk answered tersely. "Take this and keep us straight."

He handed Rose the paddle and she dipped it in the water. No, that was moving the boat toward the bank. There, that was better.

She watched in horror as four of the wedewolves waded into the water. At the point where it curved around the stand of trees, the river's current slowed down significantly, enough to make it possible for them to swim. With their numbers, they could easily overwhelm the boat and pull the two humans into the water to finish them off.

All ten of the wedewolves were now in the water. Powerful legs propelled them toward the middle of the river, where they stopped and swam in place as they waited for the boat to come to them. It wouldn't take long. Rose shuddered abruptly. Benk wouldn't have time to kill all of them. The narrow heads slitting through the water weren't much of a target.

Suddenly she was sick and tired of wedewolves.

"Go away!" she shouted furiously.

There was the twang of Benk's bow behind her. One of the wedewolves lurched in the water, an arrow through its head. Another twang; then another, and two more were killed.

The wedewolves had underestimated their archer.

The sturdy bow behind Rose kept twanging its song of death. She couldn't believe it. Each arrow that flew from Benk's bow went straight to the head of a wedewolf. Four. Five. Six. The river that had slowed down to accommodate the wedewolves was proving to be their undoing. They couldn't swim as fast as they could run, though they were swimming as hard as they could to get out of the water. Seven. The last three had almost made it to the bank of the river. Eight. Nine.

"One more to go. You can do it, Benk!"

The last wedewolf leaped from the water and streaked away, head lowered and body a blur. Twang went the bow and the tenth wedewolf fell, an arrow through its head.

Rose's mouth fell open. She stared at the dead bodies of the wedewolves half-sinking, half-floating in the water as the current carried their boat on down the river. Then she twisted around and stared at Benk. He was leaning down, putting the bow back into his backpack where it would stay dry. When he straightened up again, their eyes met. For a long minute Rose stared wordlessly at him.

Benk shrugged and reached for the paddle.

"Waste of good arrows."

"Not a waste," Rose said.

She handed him the paddle and faced the front of the boat again. A minute later she muttered, "Thank you."

"Any time," Benk answered lightly.

They traveled the rest of that afternoon in silence. Towards evening there was a loud splashing sound up ahead. Benk paddled the boat toward the shore and tied it to a conveniently protruding tree root.

"I'll check on what's there," he said and jumped onto the shore.

Rose sat frowning at her feet. She didn't need the numbing salve as much anymore, which was a good thing since they'd almost scraped the container empty. Nevertheless, her feet hurt if she bumped them against anything and she hadn't tried walking. She didn't know if she could.

"I hate being helpless. Are you even listening?"

She didn't say a name. It wasn't necessary—the Maker would know she was talking to him. She wondered how long he'd put up with her.

"One demand after another, but what else can I do?"

As soon as she asked the question, Rose knew what Nurse B would tell her.

"Think of the things he's already done for you, child. List them in your head. That will help you ask for what you need with a proper attitude."

Rose could practically hear her nurse. The impatience in her words would be more than balanced by the love, but it hurt too much to think of Nurse Broomely. She needed to think of something else. *Where are we going?* Benk would know. She'd ask him when he got back.

Without warning, grass rustled close by. She cowered down in the boat. Benk hadn't rustled any grass when he left. This was a large animal and there was nothing she could do to protect herself. When Benk emerged from the trees, she drew a deep sobbing breath.

"What's the matter? I made noise coming back so I wouldn't surprise you."

"It didn't work. I was surprised," Rose scolded. *And scared,* she added to herself.

The scout stepped into the water alongside the boat and rummaged in her backpack.

"That's MY backpack."

He ignored her until he found the rope ladder. Then he explained, "There are rapids up ahead. I'd rather go through them in the morning."

Rose shook her head. "But it's only late afternoon. There'll be plenty of light for two or three hours."

"The wedewolves are dead. We don't have to take chances anymore," Benk told her shortly.

"I know they're dead," she grumbled, though it was quite true that she had an irrational desire to get as far away from them as possible. Then she straightened.

"Oh-h-h-h, I get it. You're tired!"

He ignored her but Rose knew she was right. *And no wonder,* she thought but couldn't make herself say it. Besides, she had something new to worry about. Benk was studying the tree limbs above them.

"I can't climb the rope ladder. My feet—"

"You won't have to," he interrupted, continuing to look at the tree.

He found a branch he liked and threw the rope towards it. Rose noted with satisfaction that it took him three throws before he got the rope to go around the branch and drop back down. She could have done that.

Quickly the scout pulled the ladder up to the branch and secured it. He strapped his heavy pack on and climbed the ladder. Tying his pack to the tree, he came down to do the same thing for Rose's pack. Then he motioned to Rose.

"Put your feet over the side of the boat and slide onto my back," he ordered as he turned and crouched.

Rose shook her head again. "It won't work. I'm heavier than a pack and—"

"Do you want to bathe first?" he asked, facing her with a glint in his eyes. He was obviously not in the mood for arguments. "I could get the bar of soap for you."

"No," she answered automatically.

"Then I promise you that your weight will not be the worst part of the climb for me," he said turning around once more and motioning with his hand.

For the first time, Rose was embarrassed by her dirty, smelly body. She leaned forward and grabbed his shoulders with her hands.

"Put your arms around my neck but don't cut off my breathing. That's right. Now wrap your legs around my waist."

This is the most humiliating experience of my life, Rose decided halfway up the ladder.

———— ⚇ ————

Benk was panting when he reached the top, but he made it. There was an awkward moment while the girl on his back transferred her grip to a tree branch. He was ready to grab her if she started to fall but she didn't. Undoubtedly that was a good thing. Even at the risk of falling out of a tree, she wouldn't have liked him grabbing her.

Soon they were both lying in hammocks, gazing through leaves to a blue sky and enjoying the breeze that blew first over Benk and then Rose. The scout had hung their hammocks with wind direction in mind. He took a deep breath of fresh air, congratulating himself on his foresight.

"I'm wondering why you have two hammocks," he mentioned eventually.

Rose hesitated as if she wasn't going to tell him. Then she sighed.

"My mother died when I was born. Everyone hated me because of her death; everyone but my nurse. Nurse Broomely took me to her farm and raised me until they made us go back to the castle. I packed two hammocks because I didn't want to leave without her."

"Why did you?" Benk asked softly.

He had wondered what gave this girl her sharpness.

"Nurse B died," Rose spoke into the leaves above her head. Her grief was in her voice.

"I'm sorry," he responded but she continued as if she hadn't heard him.

"I had to leave. They were going to make me marry. They were horrible."

Benk nodded. "I've heard about the Yospaldon court, but if they didn't like you why would they care if you left?"

"I was an untouchable princess. Someone would have paid a lot of money to marry me," she said wearily.

Benk mused over that for a while. Marrying a woman off to the highest bidder was contemptable, but he couldn't help wondering who would want to touch, much less marry, an awful-smelling girl with greasy hair.

"And your name was?" he asked slyly, thinking that they'd talked seriously enough for one night.

Rose smiled at the leaves above her. "You're tricky!"

"The wedewolves thought so. Twelve arrows for twelve wedewolves; told you I could," he bragged.

"Lucky shots," she argued but she was still smiling.

The next morning Rose didn't fuss when Benk carried her down the rope ladder. She couldn't help but see that his face was tight with the effort not to breathe any more than necessary. They ate dried food from her pack before shoving off the bank into the river. The rapids ahead didn't seem to be any problem for the scout. He maneuvered through them with ease and by mid-morning they had reached a fork in the river. Benk steered them to the right without hesitation.

"We'll head west toward my kingdom, Far Reaches. I'd like Windola to take a look at your feet. She's the best healer I know."

"Do you think she can heal them?" Rose asked bluntly.

"I don't know but she's very good with herbs. She's the one who gave me the numbing salve."

That wasn't the definite reassurance she wanted, but at least she knew now where they were going. She just wished it wouldn't take such a long time to get there. Watching for logs in the river was losing its novelty. By the time they pulled over for the night, Rose had made a decision. It was Benk's turn to talk. She waited until after supper and then started in on him.

"You were breathing hard after you took me up the rope ladder. I don't understand how you could have carried me down the mountain to the cabin—and if I'm remembering right, you've always said 'we' when you talked about it. Who else was there? Was it that Yospaldon who told you about me?"

Benk stared into the fire at first. Rose didn't like being ignored. She was opening her mouth to say something snappish when he answered.

"It wasn't the Yospaldon. He was taking a big risk meeting me at all. After passing on the news, he left. My horse carried you and me down the mountain. The wedewolves were on our trail towards the end, but they didn't catch up until after we'd reached the cabin and I'd told Redder to leave."

"Redder was the name of your horse? Redder? As in more red?"

Benk's face lightened a bit. "I was young when I started training him. He was a bay, which means—"

"I know—black mane and tail, red body."

"A lot of the other scouts' horses were bays. I might have mentioned a few times that my horse's coat was redder than any of theirs. The name stuck."

"Might have?" Rose asked insinuatingly.

"I've heard it said that I was a bit cocky back then."

Rose threw her hands up and proclaimed to the world, "COCKY! That was the word I was trying to think of. It describes you perfectly. Where did Redder go when you told him to leave?"

The scout's face darkened.

"He didn't make it. The next day I looked out the window and saw two wedewolves quarreling over a hunk of meat with long black hair attached to it. The black hair was part of Redder's mane."

Benk stopped. There was a dead silence.

"I didn't know," Rose whispered. It was a totally inadequate thing to say. She wiped a few tears from her eyes.

Benk rubbed his face with the back of one hand.

"It's not your fault," he said gently, and it was his kindness that broke her down.

"Yes, it is. It's my fault Redder died, and it's my fault Nurse Broomely had to go to the Yospaldon palace and die in that awful place. It'll be my fault if Ricaldo dies for helping me, and if that Yospaldon—"

Benk interrupted her. He was still gentle, but he was also firm.

"It's not your fault. You're not responsible for the Yospaldons or the wedewolves. Neither are you responsible for the Maker's people who helped you. It was their choice, not yours, and if they die, they go to the high home. To say it's a much better place is an understatement."

Rose's face slowly untwisted. She took a deep shuddering breath. Benk doused the fire and got out the rope ladder.

"The wedewolves are dead, but it's safer in a tree. We shouldn't take chances."

The scout got the rope ladder over a tree branch on his first try. He pulled the ladder up and threw the rope expertly around the branch two more times. He carried up his backpack and then he carried up her backpack. Then he carried up the smelly, lumpy girl. They attached their hammocks and lay down quietly.

Several minutes later the smelly, lumpy girl spoke.

"Benk?"

"Yeah?"

"My name is Rose."

Chapter 7

PEOPLE!

Benk kept their boat in the fastest part of the current the next three days, paddling constantly to speed them up even more. He told Rose he was hurrying because their food supplies wouldn't last forever and he didn't want to take the time to hunt or fish, but she didn't think he was telling the whole truth.

Her feet weren't healing. Every morning and evening Benk inspected them, but he never said anything and his face was always unreadable. That had to be a bad sign. If they were getting better, he would have told her.

Early on the fourth day, the main current started running through a deep trough that wound from one side of the river to the other. Rose winced every time they came close to the river's bank. *The wedewolves are dead*, she reminded herself but it didn't make any difference. As soon as the current changed directions and took them across to the other bank, she immediately winced again.

Benk noticed, of course.

He started making solemn statements about killer frogs and dangerous bugs, and every statement got more and more ridiculous. Rose groaned, trying to discourage him. He kept it up. When he made such an outlandish remark that she couldn't help but shake with laughter, he crowed in triumph.

All in all, it was a good morning—until a little after noon.

That was when they passed a bear fishing in the water on one side. Fortunately the current was taking them through the middle of the river at that point. Their boat passed close enough as it was. The bear stood on its two shaggy hind legs and watched them go by. He was thirteen feet tall. His paws were as big as baskets, hairy baskets with eight-inch claws.

"We're fortunate it wasn't a mother with cubs. Females are so emotional and moody," Benk remarked after they'd passed.

Rose didn't reply to this thinly-veiled insult, because her heart was beating as if it meant to jump out of her body and power-swim away. It wasn't that she hadn't seen bears before. They had visited the apple trees on Nurse B's farm every fall when the fruit was ripe. She'd always enjoyed watching them from a safe distance.

This bear had been ten feet away, and it had been bigger than any animal she'd ever seen. Several minutes passed before her heartbeat slowed down. Then she let Benk have it.

"That bear was getting along in years. It's a pity males bulge so in the middle as they age."

Benk roared with laughter and continued to laugh off and on for the next hour. Rose grinned every time he laughed, though she was careful not to let him see her do it. She didn't know why. *It's hard to break old habits.*

Late in the afternoon, the scout slowed the boat down and stared at the river, which was curving toward the east.

"We're not going the right direction anymore. This part of Montaland is north of the Kingdom of Mount Pasture where I grew up. I want to take you to Far Reaches and let Windola work on your feet, but it makes sense to borrow horses at Mount Pasture. Do you think you could walk if I make you shoes with moss for cushioning?"

"I could try," Rose agreed, though her words wobbled and

her hands snuck down to grab at the wooden board she was sitting on.

It wasn't the prospect of walking on sore feet that made her uneasy. At least it wasn't only that. Benk had added the Kingdom of Mount Pasture to their plan and that meant more people. Rose didn't like people. She cleared her throat and tried to talk without a wobble.

"Yospaldo wasn't a very good kingdom, but it's all I know. Tell me about Mount Pasture and Far Reaches."

"Mount Pasture is sheep and Far Reaches is scouts," Benk answered as he paddled the boat toward the shore.

Rose waited—and waited. Benk tied the boat to a tree when it had gone as far into the shallow water as it could go.

"I was actually expecting a little more information than that," she finally commented dryly, and he snickered.

"You want to know more? All right, but let me find the moss I need first."

Rose watched him leave and then rubbed her feet very gently even though they hurt at the touch. She was tired of being helpless. Gritting her teeth, she wondered if she could get out of the boat by herself, but before she could try Benk returned with his hands full.

"I didn't have to go far. There was moss on the edges of a nearby creek and a tree with the right kind of bark growing next to it."

"What's the right kind of bark?" asked Rose, interested in this wilderness shoe-making.

"Any kind that peels off in a long strip," Benk answered absently. He was absorbed in his task and Rose left him alone, though she hung over the side of the boat and watched.

"Done," he said in a few minutes.

He sloshed through the water and picked her up, his face tightening as it always did when he came near her. Gently he placed her on top of a log and tied the makeshift shoes around her feet. It hurt.

"If I weren't such a polite girl, what a kick in the face I would give you."

He answered without looking up. "Better not. I might dunk you in the water and start scrubbing."

"You wouldn't dare!"

He straightened. "You won't get a chance to find out. The shoes are on. Take my hand and we'll see how they work."

Hesitantly Rose stood on her feet. It had been a long time since she'd put any weight on them. She took a tentative step.

"I think I can do it," was what she said, but there was a tiny pucker between her eyes and her lips made the slightest of movements toward a grimace.

Benk noticed again. Scouts were annoyingly observant people—helpful at times, but annoying all the same.

"We'll take it easy. There's a waterfall a short distance ahead. It's one of my favorite places. You'll like it."

Every step was painful, but Rose couldn't believe how good it felt to be walking again. It even felt good to wear her pack. Benk had transferred all the heavy things to his backpack, but carrying something made her feel useful.

I'm free, she exulted as she hobbled up a slight slope. *Well, kind of.*

Twenty minutes passed, and Rose began to wonder where the waterfall was.

"What do you mean by 'a short distance?'" she asked Benk, but instead of answering he stopped to gaze intently in front of them.

"What is it?"

"I think we may have company."

Rose studied the stretch of woods they were entering. It didn't seem any different to her, but she wasn't a scout. If Benk said someone had passed that way, they probably had.

"That's too bad. Where else can we go?" she asked and he shook his head at her.

"We'll go to the waterfall. There's no need to be afraid

this far from Yospaldo."

Rose didn't respond. She started walking when Benk did and tried to control her tension.

"You forgot to tell me about the other kingdoms," she said, hoping that would help her relax.

"So I did. Well, Mount Pasture has lower hills than most of Montaland and—"

Abruptly he stopped walking again and stared at a tree to their right. Then he chuckled.

"Perfect," he said.

Rose stared at the tree. It was a tree; that much she could tell, but she refused to ask what was going on again. She was tired of asking questions. Maybe she was just tired. Her feet hurt. She was shifting weight from one to the other, when Benk pursed up his lips and whistled a perfect imitation of a bird's song.

"Now what are you doing?"

Rose couldn't help speaking impatiently. It was fine to stop and make birdcalls, and Benk did it very nicely, but she wanted to get to a place where she could take the weight off her feet.

"Mountain wren."

"That's not what I meant," she told him with a sigh, but Benk was chuckling once more.

A bird was calling from somewhere in front of them. A second bird warbled as soon as the first one stopped. They weren't very good calls. Even Rose could tell they were imitations. Two boys suddenly darted over the top of a slope and hurtled toward them.

"Benk!" they yelled, and he shouted back in delight.

Then there was a whole group of bodies running toward them and the excitement of friends meeting in an unexpected place.

It wasn't until everyone had arrived at a camping place and sat around a fire that Rose began sorting out the newcomers. Largen and Tuff told her how old they were before they told her their names. They were twelve and eleven, and proud of it. Alissa was the oldest girl and bossy toward her little sister, Iris.

"Alissa is nine and Iris is six," someone said next to her.

Rose turned to find a woman handing her a cup of cold water. The woman had green eyes, long brown hair tied back with a ribbon, and a face that Rose liked.

"Petten is my husband," the woman continued, indicating an attractive man with curly hair. "He's older than I am though he doesn't look it. I have to tell people."

"Not true," Petten disagreed.

"Oh yes, it is. Sad but true." She smiled at Rose. "I'm Janna, and I've known Benk since he was born. He cheats at tag."

"I do not," Benk defended himself mildly, but Janna waved a hand toward him in airy dismissal.

"What's your name?" several people asked Rose.

Rose had to make herself tell them her name. These were obviously people she could trust. Why was it hard to tell them her name?

Janna was smiling at Iris.

"Another flower name," she pointed out.

"But Mama, she stinks!" said Iris, holding a hand over her nose.

Rose's face flamed. She could imagine what she smelled like after all this time.

"Iris!" scolded Janna, Petten, and Alissa at the same time, but it was Alissa who added, "You're not supposed to say things like that even if they're true."

Janna groaned at both girls and told Rose contritely, "I'm sorry."

"It's all right," Rose mumbled awkwardly, hoping she wouldn't burp. This was the kind of situation that had always made her burp back in Yospaldo. "I know I smell awful. Benk has been rushing us and I haven't had time to bathe."

A choking sound came from Benk's direction, making

some of the tension leave Rose. Maybe she wouldn't burp after all.

Alissa took charge. "We were going swimming. Why don't you come with us?"

"I'd love to," Rose agreed, and a repeat of the choking sound put a smile on her face.

"We men will take a turn after you ladies are done," Petten said, looking hard at his boys, who didn't seem to like the arrangement.

They were probably going to swim as a family. Rose stood up gingerly and glanced at Benk. The incredulous expression on his face gave her a little sorely needed confidence.

"Come on," shouted Alissa and Iris, and she started to follow them, trying not to flinch at the pain.

"My feet are hurt. I'll have to go slower than you," she explained.

"What happened to your feet?" asked Janna who had slowed down to walk beside her.

It was then that Benk found his voice.

"If I were you, I'd take that stomach thing off and bury it!" he called after them loudly.

Rose jerked her head around. "How do you know about my middle?"

Benk answered calmly, but Rose could see his eyes were laughing even at a distance. "I brought you down the mountain. I've always known about it. I know you're not a fourteen-year-old too. How old are you really?"

"S-seventeen," she stammered.

"Why the lie?"

"I told everyone I was fourteen because I didn't want to get married off. It wasn't a lie. I am fourteen—plus three years. You didn't say anything," she finished blankly.

He snorted sarcastically. "Oh yeah, saying something would have been a good idea. You trusted me right from the start."

She stared at him, dumbfounded, until Janna took her arm.

"The sooner we leave, the sooner we'll be back," the older woman said, making a face at Benk.

The waterfall wasn't a large one, but it splashed into a pool that was fringed on either side by small trailing plants with white flowers. *Beautiful*! Rose wanted to study it but there wasn't time. The girls had already taken their clothes off down to their underwear and were bobbing and shrieking with glee in the cold water.

"We leave our underthings on and wash them at the same time we wash ourselves," Janna said.

"I can't wait," Rose assured her and it was true. She was tired of being filthy. In short order she'd tugged her dress over her head and tried to untie the middle, but day after day of sweat had gotten into the knot, making it hard to undo. Janna had to come and help her.

"There's a reason for this, I'm sure," the older woman said as she worked at the stubborn knot. "However, I suggest we bathe first and talk afterwards. Ah, here we go."

The middle was unceremoniously tossed under the nearest bush, and Rose gingerly massaged the skin on her stomach that was chafed from having rubbed against it for so long. Then she pulled off the makeshift shoes and walked into the water. Her feet throbbed with pain, but she ignored them. Janna handed her a bottle when she was deep enough, and Rose had to use over half of the shampoo to get her hair clean. She felt guilty, but Janna wasn't troubled.

"It's useful to marry a scout; it really is. Petten knows what to find in the wilderness for any need. If we run out of shampoo, he'll find something that can substitute, and the kids will like it better than what I brought!"

"Benk knows a lot too," Rose said and then stopped, overcome with embarrassment once more, but Janna paid no attention to her red face.

She was trying to brush Rose's hair. There was a tangle

half-way down her back that wouldn't brush out. They gave it up for the time being, and Rose sat in a shallow part of the pool and soaped herself thoroughly—except for her feet, which she couldn't bring herself to touch. Hopefully they would soak clean. The rest of her was certainly clean and glowing when she was done. Hobbling from the water, she sat on a rock while Janna examined her feet. The serious expression that crossed the older woman's face was no surprise to Rose.

"I know they're bad. I hope Benk's healer can do something."

"Nothing I brought will help," Janna admitted. She tilted her head thoughtfully. "Benk must be taking you to Windola. There's no one on Montaland who knows more about herbs and roots than Windola."

"That's what I heard," agreed Rose as she picked up the brush and tried again to straighten the tangle in the back of her hair. She worked on it for five minutes before giving up. Her arms were aching. Janna took another turn, but eventually she stopped too.

"This isn't going to untangle. Do you mind if we—"

"Chop it off," Rose said with a shrug.

"Alissa, run back to your Dad and ask him for my scissors. He'll know where they are. Then walk back. Did you hear me? When you come back with those scissors in your hands, walk!"

Alissa and Iris had finished their swim and dressed long ago, but the detangling process had been too interesting to leave, even for a campfire. After Alissa ran off importantly, Rose noticed Iris staring at her.

"Your hair's drying pretty," the little girl said.

Rose hesitated before she responded, "Thanks," but she must have looked her confusion, because Iris glanced questioningly at her mother.

"I've spent so long trying to be ugly that I don't know how to be anything else. I could almost welcome that middle back on if it wasn't so smelly," Rose explained.

"No!" Janna and Iris both insisted at the same time and all three laughed.

Then Alissa came back with the scissors and Janna went to work. When the tangle was removed, the rest had to be cut the same length. In the end her hair hung an inch below her shoulders.

"Don't worry. It's still long," Alissa assured her.

The Yospaldon ladies prided themselves on the length of their hair, whether it was wound around their heads or left to swing free. Rose and Nurse Broomely had added blotches to Rose's face and a middle to her waist, but they had never dared cut her hair.

"I don't care how long my hair is," Rose said. The less she looked like the Yospaldon women, the better.

Janna picked up Rose's dress and held it in front of her. Rose hadn't paid any attention to it since she'd put it on for the Welcome to Spring Reception in Yospaldo. The dress had been unattractive then. It had not improved with time.

"What are those purple things?" Iris asked,

Rose responded frankly. "Ugly flowers, but I don't have anything else to wear. I'll clean it and—"

Janna interrupted her.

"Iris, it's your turn now. Run back and tell Petten to give you my other dress. It's at the bottom of my backpack. Don't even try to talk me out of it, Rose. No one could wear this thing. I wouldn't make rags from it. We'll let the boys bury both it and that stomach thing."

Janna tossed the dress into the bushes next to the despised middle and in a few minutes, Rose was wearing the extra dress. Although a bit large for her, the deep blue color was lovely, and she couldn't stop running her hands down the soft material. The two girls watched her, their heads on one side.

"You're thinner than Mama," Alissa observed.

"Now THAT will be enough of THAT," Janna corrected

her oldest daughter, with an exaggerated scowl on her face that made both girls giggle. "Some things are better left unspoken, young lady!"

Limping toward the campfire, Rose felt as if she'd lost a hundred pounds. She was looking forward to surprising Benk, but when every male face around the campfire dropped its jaw, she felt flustered.

"Isn't Rose pretty, Daddy?" Iris asked, skipping over to him and settling on his lap.

"Yes. She's almost as pretty as your mother," Petten replied.

Janna threw a potholder at him and the awkwardness passed.

As soon as the men and boys left for their swim, Janna organized preparations for supper.

"I don't know why it is, but cooking on a camping trip is much more fun than cooking at home. Everything takes twice as long and is harder to do, but it's more fun."

Janna chatted away and the girls were given easy jobs. Nevertheless, Rose felt uptight again even when Janna let her cut up the carrots and potatoes. It was frustrating. These were the friendliest people she'd ever met. *What's the matter with me?*

Then the boys returned. They raced to the campsite with handfuls of thin green branches in their hands and importantly got out their knives.

"We trim off the leaves and twigs so everyone can toast things in the fire," Largen told Rose.

Alissa put her hands on her hips. "Silly, everyone knows how to do that."

"No, I, uh, don't. What do you toast?" Rose asked self-consciously.

Largen was busy ignoring his sister, so Tuff answered, "You can toast anything. Meat, potatoes, bread, apple pieces—"

"Only you have to take the piece of apple from the heat when it's done or it becomes applesauce and falls off the stick," Janna reminded him.

"After it's toasted, you dip it in this cheese stuff," Tuff continued, undaunted by his mother's reminder of past failures.

"Cheese stuff! He means a cheese sauce that we make in a pot," Alissa said with a superior air.

Tuff scowled and Janna quickly intervened.

"That's enough, you two. Why don't you make our cheese sauce tonight?"

Everyone was working when Petten and Benk came into sight. The two men paused a short distance from the campfire while Benk told Petten something in a low voice. Rose had the distinct impression that he was talking about her. It didn't make her feel more comfortable.

Supper was a noisy, fun event. Janna placed the pot of cheese sauce right next to Rose, who managed to toast two pieces of meat and one piece of potato. Her apple fell into the fire though, and the children laughed with delight.

"The first time you do apples, they always fall off," Iris assured her.

Iris had adopted Rose. The little girl sat beside her and handed her things. Rose was frantically grateful, not only for the practical help but because Iris let her know what was expected more than once.

"You've got to try again," the little girl said now.

Rose didn't want to try again. She wanted to quit. The noise was bothering her. She'd lived alone with Nurse Broomely all her growing-up years. At the castle she'd avoided groups of people whenever possible. Noise signaled danger to her. This many people signaled danger.

"Okay," she said instead and obediently put another apple chunk on the end of her stick. This time she managed to get it away from the fire before it fell, which earned her a loud cheer from the children, who were obviously watching everything she did. Rose smiled faintly at them and ate her apple, not telling them that it was practically raw. She hadn't dared let it get soft.

After supper the family cleaned up with loud shouts and equally loud jokes. When Benk walked over to the log she had moved to, Rose was breathing fast and holding onto the log as if it might run away if she let it go.

"I need to check your feet."

"They're fine," she growled.

She wished everyone would leave her feet alone. In fact she wished they'd leave her alone, and the impossibility of such a thing made her irritable. A muscle twitched in Benk's face. Rose could tell he was angry. She stared at the ground and willed herself not to say anything nasty.

"Tomorrow we will leave one of the nicest families in Montaland and head toward the Kingdom of Mount Pasture. I need to see how the walk today affected your feet in order to judge how far we can go."

Benk wasn't trying to hide his anger. His words were controlled but curt.

"All right," Rose agreed in a small voice. They had almost been friends, she and Benk. Now she was ruining everything, and she didn't even understand why.

Benk squatted in front of her. "What's the matter with you?" he asked as he studied her feet.

"I don't know," she said so miserably that he glanced up at her, startled.

"Everyone's a friend here. No one's threatening you."

"Yes," Rose whispered.

Benk looked at the foot he was holding in his hand. "These sores don't look so good. I'll make a drag out of tree branches and pull you in it. Mount Pasture isn't far."

The very thought of entering a new kingdom in that way made Rose want to throw up.

"I don't want to be dragged. If you get me fresh moss for my shoes and make it thick, I think I can walk."

She clasped her hands together, willing him to understand. He eyed her, weighing the different options.

"I'll do it," he decided.

Rose smiled at him in her relief and he smiled back. Maybe their friendship hadn't been ruined.

"We're done," Alissa called as she and Largen carried a clean pot from the direction of the stream.

Tuff ran up with the washed utensils and Janna packed the cooking things.

"Storytime!" Petten announced.

"I want to hear Rose's story," Alissa said and the other children readily agreed.

Unexpectedly Janna didn't. "There's a time and place for everything. Rose has had some hard experiences, and she's tired. We need to help her relax. After all, we want to be her friends, don't we?"

The children reluctantly backed down, and Rose gazed over the campfire at Janna, almost in homage. Understanding was the last thing she'd expected to receive from a stranger. Tears were hovering, and she had to bite her tongue to keep them back.

"Tell how you and Mama met, Daddy," Iris suggested.

Petten groaned. "I've told that story a thousand times. Wouldn't you rather hear a different one?"

"No," said all the children.

"Rose hasn't heard it," Alissa pointed out.

"Well, once there was a very lovely twelve-year-old girl who was a slight bit overweight—" Petten said with a twinkle in his eye.

"Watch it, mister! That's an inconsequential fact if I ever heard one!" Janna interrupted.

"What's 'inconsequential' mean?" Iris wanted to know and Alissa, who knew everything, told her.

"It's something Mama doesn't want to talk about."

Janna fell over backwards in defeat, and everyone howled with laughter.

Rose was so relieved not to be the center of attention that she found herself enjoying the story. Nevertheless, she was glad when Petten ended it and sent the children off to their sleeping bags. Benk reached for Rose's pack and pulled her blanket out. He handed it to her with a grin.

"No tree ladder tonight."

"Good."

Rose yawned and crawled a few feet from the fire before wrapping the blanket around her and lying down.

Benk, Janna, and Petten continued talking by the fire. Rose wanted to listen in case they discussed her, but she was too tired. Her mind fuzzed over and she sank into a deep, exhausted sleep.

Chapter 8

MOUNT PASTURE AND FAR REACHES

They ate a quick breakfast the next morning. Petten wanted his family to get an early start, because for their vacation this year, they planned to travel far to the west and camp on the shores of an enormous lake. It would take them two weeks to get there, if not longer. The children told Rose enthusiastically about a water bird with long legs they hoped to see.

A water bird? They're traveling that far to see a water bird?

Rose didn't say anything, but her face must have given her away. The children shifted their attention to Benk. He was a scout—Rose figured he already knew about the big lake and stupid water bird, but he listened and cheered the children on. They responded by hugging him repeatedly as they said their goodbyes. They hugged Rose once.

I don't care.

Petten smiled at her for a goodbye and Rose was fine with that. She just wanted them to leave and be done with it, though when Janna rushed over and gave her a warm hug, she surprised herself by liking it. No one had hugged her affectionately since Nurse Broomely had died.

"I'll come and visit as soon as we get back. The Maker will

take care of you," the older woman whispered.

"I know," Rose answered automatically but she was thinking about Janna, not the Maker. She liked Janna. She felt safe with Janna. She wanted Janna to stay with her instead of going on a long trip with her husband and children. Rose watched until the family disappeared in the trees.

Then she turned to Benk, who was pulling his pack onto his shoulder. It was bulging out on the sides more than normal. And where was hers?

"I transferred everything from your pack into mine," he said when he saw her looking around.

"But where's the pack?"

"I stuffed it in last."

"I could carry something," Rose insisted, lifting her chin. She wasn't totally useless.

"No need. It might have made it worse on you yesterday, carrying the pack. Let's go."

They walked slowly through the woods. The morning was warm and there were leaves on the trees, but they were still the light green of spring. In a few days these spring leaves would deepen into all different shades of deep green. When that happened, summer would have officially arrived. Wild flowers were scattered everywhere, and Rose wished she could stop and study them. Flowers were her favorite things to embroider, but she liked to copy them exactly.

She wasn't in any hurry to get to Mount Pasture. There were people in Mount Pasture and she didn't get along with people. Unfortunately Benk didn't want to stop and study flowers. He kept them moving steadily through the woods, though Rose couldn't help but walk slower and slower as the morning wore on. The scout finally stopped in frustration.

"I could crawl faster."

"My feet hurt. If you have replacements for them, I'd be happy to let you chop these off at the ankles," she snapped.

"I don't think that will be necessary, Rose," Benk said kindly, and she glanced quickly to one side. As always, the combination of kindness and name was almost too much for her.

"Why don't I carry you piggyback?"

It was in the form of a question, but it wasn't one. It was an order. Rose wanted to stomp her feet, but that would have hurt too much. She could almost feel the hair rising on her neck. The idea of putting her arms around this man, even from the back, was appalling, especially without her middle to provide a separation. However, Benk was taking off his pack and dropping it on the ground. He leaned over.

Reluctantly Rose took hold and jumped.

"If you do anything I don't like, I'll bite your ear," she informed him.

"If you do anything I don't like, I'll tickle your stomach."

Rose subsided instantly. He had guessed correctly; she hated to be tickled. Carrying his pack in his hands, Benk strode on five times faster than they'd been going.

A half hour later, they left the woods and entered a world of pastures. Benk seemed to know where he was going and followed the wood's edge until they reached the corner of a fence. Then he turned away from the woods and followed the fence.

Rose felt as if she had been carried to the center of "green". Surrounding her in every direction was grass covering low rolling hills, but what was most noticeable to Rose was the smell. For the rest of her life she associated the color "green" with the smell of grass. She was so taken with the strangeness of being "inside green" that she forgot to wonder where they were going, even when Benk left the fence and began climbing a low rise.

He was puffing by the time they reached the top. She almost suggested stopping to give him a break, but the words caught in her throat. On the other side of the rise were several small cottages. Smoke swirled from their chimneys, and there were well-tended gardens around the nearest. Rose smiled her pleasure.

That was the last time she smiled for the remainder of her stay in Mount Pasture.

———— ∞∞ ————

Benk grinned when a plump woman with white hair twisted up on her head came bustling from the nearest cottage. She was talking as soon as she came outside—possibly before.

"Gracious highlands, Benk, how did you ever find us? You must have run into Janna and her family; they helped us move and settle in."

He answered cheerfully as he went down the hill, which was shorter on this side and much less steep.

"We met at the waterfall. How do you like being retired, Queen Berta?"

"I haven't had time to think about it, but it's not 'Queen' Berta anymore, you know. Hello, where are my manners? Are you hurt?"

"This is Rose. She's fine, except for her feet," Benk answered for her. "We need a place to stay for a few days, if that's all right."

Berta beckoned as she rushed toward the side door.

"Of course it is. Come right in. I left rolls baking that I've got to check. Then I'll see what I can do for your feet, Rose. We'll have lunch soon, and I'll invite all your brothers and sisters for supper, Benk. Alissa and Alland are sick with the spring flu, but I know they'll come if they can."

Benk followed Berta inside and let Rose down. Walking gingerly to the nearest chair, she sat down. He watched her out of the corner of his eyes. Sure enough, the first thing she did was frown heavily. Meeting new people was not her favorite thing, but she was going to have to get over that. It was going to be new people from now on.

His prediction was quite accurate: the stream of people never ended. They poured into the small house, chattering happily like water tumbling over rocks—until they saw the poor condition of Rose's feet. Then they stopped short and gave advice. Rose had a constantly grumpy expression on her face. She probably slept that way. Benk didn't care for her attitude and told her so the first time he got a chance.

"They're enjoying my hurt feet. It gives them something to talk about," she complained.

He stared at her hard enough to make her squirm, but she didn't back down.

"What king and queen would ever retire anyway? I've never heard of such a thing."

"It's the custom in Mount Pasture," Benk told her.

"Well, they don't act retired. They're constantly busy."

Benk couldn't disagree with that. Berta was always making cookies or muffins to feed her visitors, and Luff welcomed everyone as if he or she was the most important individual in the entire mountain world. The people who lived nearby came often. The people who didn't live nearby came as often as they could. It had been five full days of socializing. Benk was tired of it too, but he had no intention of sharing that with Miss Sour, who looked as if she'd swallowed a cup of vinegar.

"Luff and Berta are FRIENDLY," he said instead, emphasizing the last word. She needed to learn what it meant.

Rose shot her answer back at him. "FRIENDLY doesn't begin to describe it. They invite hordes of people to visit and every single person has to examine my feet. These people are shepherds, not healers. I wish they'd leave me alone."

The climax came on the third day when Alland and Alissa visited. Benk had gone to see them before, flu or no flu, but they hadn't felt well enough to leave home. Now that they were better, they wanted to meet Rose.

"My oldest brother and his wife are coming today," Benk warned Miss Sour that morning.

"Big deal," she growled.

Rose was in an unusually bad mood, even for her. Several

people had joined them for breakfast and examined her feet afterwards, offering their advice. A lot of it was far-fetched, Benk had to admit, especially the one that involved soaking her feet in warm cricket water. The recipe for cricket water was nauseating and involved the death of at least a hundred crickets, but the person who'd suggested it was one of the most compassionate men Benk had ever known and didn't deserve the sarcastic look Rose had given him.

"Behave," he ordered tersely as Alland's wagon drove into the yard.

Alissa was the first one in the door, and Rose stiffened at the sight of her. Benk doubted there were any Yospaldon women more beautiful than his brother's blonde, blue-eyed wife.

Rose muttered "Ugh," though it might have been "Yuck." Benk couldn't tell which it was, but either way Alissa greeted her warmly.

"You must be Rose. Benk has told me about you. I am Alissa, Janna's best friend."

Immediately Rose burped loudly. Benk felt like throwing his hands up in the air. Didn't they teach any manners at all in Yospaldo? Alland quickly asked a question, and Benk understood that his brother was trying to take the attention off Rose. It was too bad that his effort was a dismal failure.

"Scouts are always helping people in other kingdoms. What will they do about Yospaldo?" Alland asked.

"WHAT? Nobody should do anything about Yospaldo. It's a bad place. Leave it alone," Rose sputtered.

"Relax," Benk said, though he knew it wouldn't do any good.

"Tell me you're going to leave it alone," she insisted, half-rising from her chair.

"It's not my decision to make. The scouts as a whole will decide what to do."

Rose was staring at him, wide-eyed.

"How are Janna and Petten?" Alissa asked her gently.

"Fine," Rose said numbly.

"Were the children enjoying the camping trip?" Alland asked next, and that was a much more successful question.

They talked about fires and sleeping on the ground and birdcalls for a while. Then the two visitors wisely excused themselves. Benk walked outside with them. Once they were in the yard with the door closed, he turned to Alissa.

"I told you she was difficult. I'm sorry she was rude to you."

"It's all right," Alissa said, touching his shoulder and smiling.

Alland was shaking his head, but he wasn't thinking about Rose.

"The scouts are not going to leave Yospaldo alone—and you'll be in the thick of it," he predicted, his forehead creased with worry.

⸻

As soon as the two brothers and Alissa went out the door, Rose wilted. She knew Benk was angry with her again, but she hadn't been able to control herself. Even she didn't know why that burp had come. She hadn't burped like that since leaving Yospaldo, and she'd only burped there when she felt tense. It had been as if—well, it had almost been as if—

"Jealous," she admitted.

She'd been so jealous she could hardly speak. Petten had mentioned Alissa when he told the story of how he and Janna met, but it was one thing to hear about a person in a story and another thing altogether to meet that person in real life. The whole situation was ridiculous anyway. Alissa was too old to have best friends and be beautiful, not that Rose cared about beauty. There had been lots of beautiful women in the Yospaldon castle, and they'd been the worst of the lot in her opinion. No, Alissa could have her looks. Rose didn't want them.

It was the best friend part that had tightened the muscles

in her stomach until it felt like a clenched fist. Maybe Alissa was lying. The beautiful Yospaldon women had lied. Actually all the Yospaldon women had lied, but the beautiful ones had gotten away with it more often. *She's lying*, Rose told herself, but she wasn't convinced and her shoulders drooped. Janna had named her first baby girl after this woman. That was what a best friend would do, so it must be true. Alissa was Janna's best friend and Rose was left out.

Berta was a very good cook. However, over the next two days, Rose was too unhappy to eat. Though the food looked and smelled delicious, she picked her way through each meal. Berta fussed and clucked over how little she ate. Then the older woman made something special for the next meal, which Rose picked her way through too, causing the fussing and clucking to begin again. It was irritating.

Another irritating thing was that Benk left right after breakfast every morning and didn't come back for the rest of the day. Supposedly he was finding horses for them to borrow, but how many days did it take to find two horses? Luff explained that Mount Pasture sheep herders didn't have many horses, and the ones they had were generally needed for farm work, but Rose suspected Benk was using the horse hunt as an excuse to visit old friends.

She had tension-induced hiccups all one afternoon.

Finally the morning of their departure arrived. Rose limped out of the house by herself, refusing everyone's offers of help. Grimacing as she stepped down from the porch, she hobbled over to the horse Benk had found for her. Benk fastened the strap of the bridle and turned to her without a glimmer of a smile. When he put his hands on her waist to lift her onto the horse's back, she started to snap at him, but a glint in his eyes made her stifle it.

Once she was sitting on the horse, Rose felt better. She didn't need to worry about bumping her feet on the stirrups because Benk had taken them off the saddle. Her knees would have to tighten enough to keep her on the horse; however, that was okay. Her form might not have been up to Yospaldon standards, but she had learned to ride bareback and was not above grabbing the saddle horn if necessary.

"Thank you for your hospitality," she stated graciously to Berta and Luff.

The older couple beamed at her words as if she were their new favorite person. They did that to everyone. It was enough to make a girl sick to her stomach, but Rose didn't say anything. She even managed to nod at them as she and Benk left. It may have been formal, but it was a nod, and she was pleased with herself.

They weren't far down the road when her spirits revived. She breathed in deeply. Summer had settled during their stay in Mount Pasture. The freshness of spring was gone, but fields of green grass were on either side of her once more, and the summertime heat had intensified their fragrance. There would be no more crowds of people staring at her— and as long as she was on a horse, she was independently mobile.

She smiled at Benk, but he wasn't looking at her. A little later she tried again, but he still wasn't looking, so she gave up and enjoyed the beauty of their ride.

The smooth dirt road wound between pastures. Many of them had flocks of sheep grazing on them; some had crops; a few had tall grass mixed with taller weeds. Rose knew what was going on there. Land needed to be left alone at times or it got worn out.

Whenever they passed a shepherd, Benk waved or spoke. Often he knew the shepherd's name. Rose never waved and she certainly didn't speak. Why should she? She didn't know any of these people. By mid-afternoon she could see the forest line ahead of them and knew that they would soon leave the Kingdom of Mount Pasture.

I'm ready, she thought, but a minute later they reached a

mass of sweet-smelling pink roses that were climbing over a gate.

"Oh Benk, can we stop a minute? I want to see those roses better."

"All the time in the world for flowers, but none for the people who've been kind to you, is that it?" the scout said, breaking his long silence.

"I didn't say anything rude," she answered in self-defense. He stared at her incredulously, and she added, "Not recently."

During the last two days of their visit, Rose had bitten back all the rude things that had come to mind. She'd been proud of her self-control.

"Besides, if this kingdom is so sociable, why didn't your king and queen come to visit me? Not that I wanted them to."

"They came the first day you were here. They were with some farmers. The queen recommended soaking your feet in warm salt water five times a day. You snubbed her, like you snubbed everyone else."

Rose's mouth fell open. "That was the queen? She looked like a commoner! How was I supposed to—"

Benk cut her off. "You were rude when you talked and rude when you withdrew. Can't you tell the difference between the people of Yospaldo and the people of Mount Pasture?"

"Of course I can, but I don't like people gawking at my feet," she snapped.

Benk stared keenly at her, too keenly. She turned her head away.

"You're pretty on the outside," he said.

When she jerked her head around to glare at him, he told her sharply, "Don't get burrs in your wool. I'm not paying you a compliment. It's your outside that's pretty. On the inside, you're ugly. Let's go. I want to get you to Far Reaches and leave you with Windola."

He kicked his horse into a canter and Rose followed

miserably. She was angry and miserable at first, but it didn't take her long to admit that Benk was right. Then she was just miserable. She didn't want to be ugly on the inside, but she couldn't find the words to tell Benk that, and she didn't know how to change.

They were silent the rest of the day. Benk led them deep into the forest before they stopped for the night. He swung easily off his horse. Rose brought one leg over the horse's back and twisted around. She had begun sliding, trying to go slowly to keep her feet from hitting the ground hard, when she felt Benk's hands around her waist. He put her on a part of the forest floor that was cushioned with pine straw.

"Thank you," she said humbly.

Benk looked surprised.

"You're welcome."

He didn't speak sharply this time, but she could tell he didn't want to talk. Her heart began to ache worse than her feet. That night Rose cried herself to sleep. She cried very quietly, and the night was too dark for Benk to see anything. He knew, however, because the next morning he was friendly again.

"Have some coffee," he said when Rose sat up.

He poured her a cup and Rose took it gratefully.

"We'll eat better on this part of our trip. Berta gave us enough food to last a month, and it won't take that long to get to Far Reaches."

"That's good," Rose responded, happy that he was talking to her again.

Pathetic, that's what you are. He's only a man slipped into her mind, but she dismissed that thought so quickly it startled her. *He's Benk.*

Over the next few days, Benk stayed friendly though he didn't try to talk about anything serious. Rose was relieved he wasn't angry with her anymore, but something was missing. In-between the battle with the wedewolves and the meeting with Janna's family, Rose and Benk had become friends. She felt an emptiness inside that would have made her snappy in the past. Now she was careful to reply pleasantly to Benk's casual remarks. Maybe he wouldn't get angry with her again.

They didn't leave the woods until the last full day of traveling. Trees had blocked whatever views there might have been from high places, but late that afternoon the horses climbed to the bald top of a ridge. Rose swallowed convulsively. Directly in front of them, a huge mountain dominated the world. Clouds drifted leisurely across its upper midsection and there was snow on its peak, even in the summer.

Benk waved at it. "That's Far Reaches. We'll be at Windola's cottage midday tomorrow."

Far Reaches didn't seem welcoming to Rose. It was too grand and majestic. They rode down the other side of the ridge and camped at the foot of the mountain. She wanted to cry herself to sleep that night but held back. Benk would know if she cried. It wasn't possible to hide anything from a scout, and she didn't want to admit that she didn't like his home.

When they started climbing early the next morning, Rose was relieved to find that the woods of Far Reaches were beautiful. The trees were a mixture of tall hardwoods: maples, beeches, oaks, and several trees that Rose couldn't identify. Shafts of golden sunlight fell through open spaces between branches and brightened the forest floor. Ferns grew everywhere and the air was delightfully cool.

"This is a lovely place," she commented almost in awe, staring around with big eyes.

"I think it is," Benk agreed, obviously pleased that she liked it.

Rose was glad she had said something right, so glad that the tears started to her eyes. *Pathetic!*

A little after noon, they entered a small clearing with a cottage in it. A woman opened the door and stood watching them approach. Her brown hair, streaked with gray, was tied at the back of her neck.

"Hello, Windola, how are you?" called Benk.

"Fine," she responded briefly.

She's not a talker, Rose realized with relief. She didn't have a good history with talkers.

Benk explained why they were there as he lifted Rose from the horse. Once inside the cottage, she sat on a couch and let Windola examine her feet. The healer had a gentle touch, but Rose had to wince more than once. Eventually Windola straightened.

"I can make a poultice that will help. Keep off your feet."

She gazed into Rose's face as though she were reading words printed on it. "Where are you staying?"

"I don't know. I don't have a home," Rose whispered.

Windola was silent, but Rose could feel the older woman studying her on the inside as thoroughly as she had studied her feet. It was a strange experience. The anger and resentment that had bubbled up easily in Mount Pasture had been deflated by Benk. All that was left was a tired sadness. *Can she see that?*

"You may stay here," the healer finally said.

"I'd like that."

Benk stood, well satisfied. "Exactly what I was going to suggest," he stated pompously.

"Were you?" Windola asked with a touch of amusement.

She glanced at Rose and the girl chuckled. As long as Benk was in the world, there would be laughter.

Benk grinned at them both.

"Rose, I leave you in good hands. Windola is the best healer I know and that's saying a lot."

Rose's heart twisted. How could he leave, just like that?

"Benk," she started and then stopped in confusion.

"I'll check on you from time to time. Make sure Windola is doing her job right," he informed her.

The healer grunted and made a shooing motion with her hands.

"Benk," Rose started again, but she didn't know how to continue. He had saved her life more than once. They'd been together for so many days. How could he leave? She wanted him to stay the whole time she was there. *That doesn't make sense. What would I do with him? Put him in a corner like a plant?*

He had paused, waiting to hear what she had to say.

"Benk, you are my friend," she blurted out. Once more it seemed to be the right thing to say.

"I'll visit," Benk said kindly. He swung up on his horse and rode away.

Benk didn't shake his head until the clearing was far behind him. Then he not only shook his head but rolled his eyes. That Yospaldon princess he had rescued could go from haughty to friendly without any notice whatsoever, and he never knew which was going to surface. She was interesting; he'd give her that. Pretty too. The village lads would take notice, but his guess was she'd put them in their place. In fact, they'd never know what hit them. It should be fun to watch.

"Yeah, I guess we're friends," he admitted.

He rode straight to the scouts' headquarters and reported. A meeting was called and most faces were somber as they left.

Benk's was the only face that remained cheerful. His new assignment might be dangerous, but he didn't mind. He had always liked a challenge. It wouldn't happen right away in any case. Others would go first and investigate the situation. While they were gone, he'd train a new horse while he helped Rose get used to life here. Then he'd leave.

Rose lived on the couch in Windola's kitchen. Lying down or sitting up were her two main options. Crawling on her hands and knees was allowed—so was pulling herself up onto her knees in a crouch. However, crawling and crouching were both awkward. Rose only resorted to them when it was absolutely necessary. There was a pitcher of water on her left in case she got thirsty and a covered container on the right for her basic needs. Windola always prepared lunch and left it next to the pitcher.

The healer was gone every day, but in the evenings she came back with seeds, leaves, roots, and something that smelled disgusting. Rose didn't want to know what it was. Windola mashed the seeds, leaves, roots, and disgusting something into a poultice. Half of the poultice went on Rose's feet, which were then wrapped in soft cloths overnight. The other half of the poultice was applied in the morning, and the feet were rewrapped with fresh clean cloths before Windola left for the day.

For the first time in her life Rose found herself alone with no one telling her what to do. She'd been by herself when she climbed the mountain behind Yospaldo, but that didn't count. Ricaldo had given her instructions where to go, what to do, and when to do it. Now she made little decisions on her own and changed them whenever she wanted. It was amazing how independent that made her feel.

She didn't get bored until the third day.

That day was like the others in most respects. Rose dozed occasionally and pondered life when she was awake— that's what she told herself she was doing anyway. She spent a large part of her time enjoying the view out the cottage windows. The sunshine was beautiful on the green ferns that grew three feet high in places. It was beautiful on the gray tree trunks that crowded in close to the cottage. The brown forest floor glowed wherever the light got through, but she especially liked the effect of sunlight on the dark green leaves and pink flowers of a rhododendron bush growing near the cottage.

Morning passed; lunch passed, and the afternoon was passing. Windola was usually back by now. Rose yawned.

"I'm more rested than I've ever been in my life." A few

lazy minutes passed. "This place oozes peacefulness." She stretched luxuriously. "I'll be able to think through things here!" Another minute passed.

"WHAT can I DO?"

"What do you want to do?" Windola asked, sticking her head in the door. Quiet as always, she'd been sitting outside in the sun sorting through the different herbs she'd gathered that day.

Rose blushed but her embarrassment didn't stop her from answering.

"I want to embroider rhododendron flowers," she said without hesitation.

"What will you need?"

"I'll need a medium-sized piece of undyed material, a large needle, scissors, and embroidery thread. I use a lot of colors in my pictures, even of the same shade. For this one I need different shades of yellow, green, pink, black, and white."

"Are there different shades of black and white?" Windola asked curiously.

"Oh yes. Some is in shadow, some is in the sun, and some is right next to another color. Each of those is different."

"I'll do my best," the older woman promised.

In the morning she walked to the closest village to get the embroidery supplies. Rose gazed out the window but the view didn't interest her this time, and she didn't want to think about life either.

"Pondering life is highly overrated," she grumbled and shifted positions on the couch, wishing Windola would hurry up.

The morning dragged on. Lunch provided a break, but the afternoon seemed unending. Rose was braiding her hair for the seventh time when Windola returned. She greeted the girl with a nod and handed her the items she'd found. The selection of colors was meager, to say the least, but there was a large amount of undyed thread. Rose held it up in approval.

"You can dye it yourself," the healer said as if reading her mind.

Windola stayed home the next day to fetch and carry. She brought the plants, roots, and bark Rose asked for and then she hung string all around the couch. Finally she boiled water in small pots and left them on the floor within reach of the couch.

Rose was able to take over from there. She crushed the dye materials and added them to the hot water in the pots. When she'd dyed the threads, she hung them on the string to dry. It was possible to make different shades of the same color by leaving some threads in the dye longer than others. By evening she was surrounded by long wet threads.

"I'm a spider. See my web."

The healer chuckled and went back to chopping vegetables for their pot of soup. Rose shifted unhappily. It had been a good day. She liked Windola and appreciated all she'd done. However the older woman hardly talked at all, and she would doubtlessly leave again in the morning.

I wish there was someone to talk to—not a crowd of people like in Mount Pasture, just a few.

"Benk said he'd drop by," she complained pettishly. She hadn't used that tone of voice in a long time.

"He will."

"I doubt it. He's forgotten me," Rose grumbled.

"No. He's coming. I saw him in the village."

Rose grunted in exasperation.

"Why didn't you tell me?"

"Don't say much," Windola admitted.

"Is that a fact?" Rose asked as if in great surprise and the two smiled at each other.

Rose's grumpiness was gone for the rest of that day, but it returned the next morning. Windola was gone as predicted, and Rose didn't have anything to do again. It had rained overnight. Moisture was in the air, and the threads hanging around her were still damp. They had to be thoroughly dry before she could work with them. When she heard a horse trot into the clearing, she bounced up and down on the couch.

"Anyone home?" Benk called as he dismounted.

"In here, Benk," answered Rose loudly.

The scout bounded into the cottage and his energy filled the room. Rose was so happy she was beaming, but that didn't stop her from scolding him.

"Where have you been? You said you'd come weeks ago."

"Missed me, huh? Actually, it's only been a few days since I left you here."

"Nine days! Nine long days!"

"Aren't you getting along with Windola? I thought you two would hit it off since you're both so quiet and moody."

Rose threw a pillow at him.

"I'm not moody," she insisted, laughing. It felt good to laugh again. "I'm not even quiet compared to Windola, but we're getting along fine. She's very good to me."

Benk stared at the colorful threads.

"I've never known her to keep such a messy cottage. Look at all these loose strings. Here, I know where she keeps her broom. I'll get rid of them in no time."

"Touch my threads and you die."

"What color will you dye me?" asked Benk innocently and Rose laughed again. She could never get the better of Benk by joking. She shouldn't even try.

"Tell me about Far Reaches," she begged next. "What's it like? I've lived here for nine days—"

"Nine long days," Benk solemnly corrected her.

"But I still don't know what the kingdom is like. I can't ask Windola. There are some things monosyllables won't cover."

"Far Reaches has cabins scattered over the mountain, with the biggest clusters of people living near three villages," Benk explained, settling down on a kitchen chair. "We used to have a king—it was Petten's father, as a matter of fact, but when he died, Petten didn't want to be king. He suggested we form a council to make decisions with a representative from the scouts as well as from each village. By the way, specialty workers live in the villages. Windola was looking into a place for you at the craft shop."

Rose had pursed her lips at the idea of a person not wanting to be king. She had never heard of such a thing and wondered if Petten might be mentally ill. He had seemed all right when she met him but ... Then Benk said his last few words and all questions about Petten's mental stability disappeared from her mind.

"She was? Could I embroider pictures and sell them? Where would I live?"

"Didn't she tell you? No, don't answer that. I forgot we were discussing Windola, the 'why-talk-when-it's-not-necessary' woman. Maybe she wanted them to see your work before you got your hopes up. They assured her that if you were any good, they'd be happy to sell your embroidered pictures. You'd live in the Girls' Hut."

"THE WHAT? I don't want to live there."

Benk groaned. "You don't know a thing about it and you've already made up your mind."

"So tell me," Rose ordered, sniffing haughtily.

Benk eyed her with amusement.

"There are houses for single men in the two other Far Reaches' villages, but neither of them is as large as the Girls' Hut. Females of all ages live there despite the youthful sounding name. It's for anyone who doesn't want to live by herself. The name 'hut' is misleading. The house is huge with big bedrooms that the women share with each other."

"SHARE A BEDROOM? I don't want to live there."

Benk sighed loudly.

Chapter 9

THE GIRLS' HUT

Later that day after Benk had gone, Rose repeated her announcement to Windola. "I don't want to live in the Girls' Hut."

"Why not?" Windola asked, sitting down and watching her.

Rose found it disconcerting whenever Windola looked at her in that focused manner. The older woman took in more than mere words. It made it pointless to say anything but the absolute truth.

"I don't get along with people. They don't like me."

Windola watched her a little longer and then leaned forward.

"Give the Maker a chance."

Rose's spine stiffened. "What?" she asked sharply and then caught herself. Why was she reacting in this way?

"Talk to him."

The healer stood as if the matter was closed and walked outside, leaving her patient fuming on her couch. Rose was so upset her ears felt hot.

That woman is the most infuriating person in Montaland. Telling me to talk to the Maker and then leaving before I could tell her why I didn't want to. All right! I WILL talk to the Maker and I hope you're listening because I've got plenty to say. Why didn't you give me a good life, like the people in Far Reaches or even Mount Pasture? Why did I have such a hard time? You got me away from Yospaldo, I'll give you that, but I'm crippled for life. You don't love me like you love other people.

On and on into the night, she railed. When Windola came in and went to her bedroom, Rose barely noticed. Neither did she notice pulling up the comforter at the foot of her couch when the night breezes cooled. At last she took a deep shuddering breath. Talk to the Maker! Well, she'd done it. She'd told him all the bitter angry things she could think of—and then she'd repeated them several times. Lying down on the couch, she stared into the night, eyes wide open.

I love you.

The words were inside her, but she hadn't said them. They soothed her spirit as much as the poultice soothed her feet. Sobs pushed into her throat, but they were too loud. She hushed herself and listened.

I love you, Rose.

Again the words soothed, though they were like the poultice in another respect too. They made Rose feel better for a while. Then she needed them again. Each time she listened for them, they were there, and the words of love calmed and quieted her hurting heart. Finally she pulled the comforter close enough to feel its softness against her face. Closing her eyes, she started to drift off to sleep, but before she did, she murmured, "I love you too."

The following morning, Windola took the poultice off as usual, but this time she said matter-of-factly, "You can walk now."

"Really?" Rose asked incredulously.

"Try it."

Rose swung her legs over the side of the couch and placed her feet on the floor. She winced because she was expecting the touch to be painful. It wasn't. The soles of her feet were tender, but they didn't hurt. Cautiously she put more weight on them and pushed herself up. She was standing on her feet and they felt fine.

"They're getting better!" she shouted and burst into tears.

Windola stared at her.

"Didn't you know they were better?"

"No. They didn't hurt as much, but I was convinced I'd be an invalid for life."

Windola took a deep breath.

"I'm sorry. I should have told you."

With the tears rolling down her cheeks, Rose took one tentative step after another until she was standing in front of the healer.

"You have given me back my feet. You don't have to be sorry about anything," she told her emotionally and hiccupped—but only once this time.

Windola smiled. "Will your embroidery be done in five days?"

"Are you going to the village then?" Rose asked, wiping her face dry.

Windola nodded.

"It'll be ready," Rose vowed, walking back to her couch. When she sat down and lifted her feet up, the healer nodded her approval. It was equivalent to a "don't overdo" speech from anyone else.

The next few days were busy ones. Rose worked on her picture morning and afternoon. Every now and then she walked around the kitchen. When Windola said she could go outside, she slipped on the shoes the healer had provided and walked around the clearing for the first time. In a private place behind the cottage, she sank onto the ground and leaned against a tree.

I didn't think I'd ever ... She closed her eyes and felt the warm sun on her face. *It's ... I don't know how ... It's ... I am very ...*

Rose stopped and swallowed hard. She didn't want to cry now; she wanted to be happy. Hopefully the Maker would understand her garbled thoughts and know she was trying to thank him.

Windola didn't see the finished picture until the day before she returned to the village. When Rose handed it to her, the older woman silently studied it.

"Do you like it?" asked Rose who had learned to ask if she wanted words.

"It's beautiful. It's very beautiful!"

"You said the same word twice! I couldn't get higher praise than that," squealed Rose, who was so keyed up with excitement that she had a hard time sleeping that night.

Early the next morning Windola left with the picture, and Rose's excitement left with her. She wandered through the door into the clearing, but as soon as she got a few steps outside, she wandered back in. *I want to go to the village and embroider. Even though it means living with people who won't like me.*

Cleaning up what was left of her embroidery threads didn't take long. She made herself take a walk. Afterwards she ate lunch early, hoping that would somehow speed the day along. On the same principle, she started their supper soup early. Windola made a lot of soups using herbs and vegetables.

"I'm sick of soup. I wonder ... can I remember how to make bread?"

Rose stirred flour, yeast softened in water, a little salt, and some honey together in a big bowl, hoping she'd included all the ingredients. It had been a long time since she'd made bread in Nurse B's farmhouse. She kneaded the mixture into dough on the table, put the dough into the bowl again, and then carefully placed the bowl in the oven part of the wood stove. Dough needed a warm place to rise and the oven was still warm from breakfast. It was perfect.

Flour had flown everywhere while she kneaded, so she dusted and swept. After she'd finished, the kitchen looked fresh and clean. Rose looked around with satisfaction and decided to sit and rest while her dough rose—but first she'd get the wood laid in the fire pit for later in the afternoon.

One log went in the front and one in the back, with a pile of kindling between them and bigger sticks across the kindling. Carefully balancing two small logs on top of the sticks, she brushed her hands off with satisfaction. When the kindling lit, it would light the bigger sticks, and then the bigger sticks would light the logs.

The fire lit beautifully, and Rose was headed toward her couch to rest when she came to an abrupt halt. Her dough needed to rise. If it baked now, it would cook into a hard lump.

"I didn't mean to light that fire yet," she yelped, making an awkward dash back to the stove. Her feet weren't quite up to dashing.

Grabbing the bowl of dough out of the oven, she set it on the windowsill in the sun. The rest of the afternoon dragged by. Rose baked her bread and placed it on the table with Windola's little dish of butter and a jar of wild blueberry jam. When her soup was ready, she moved it away from the heat so the vegetables wouldn't turn to mush.

To her relief Windola arrived home not long after that. She stood in the doorway and sniffed appreciatively.

"Smells good," she told Rose who was waiting anxiously.

"Did they like it?" Rose asked in an unnaturally high voice.

"They liked it."

"Will they let me work with them?"

"Yes."

Rose waited. The healer went over to the soup and stirred it.

"Windola, you need to tell me more."

"Oh. They'll hang it in the shop window after they get it framed. They want you to make more."

Rose beamed. "That's good, but they can't have that one."

Windola looked her way with a question in her eyes.

"That one's for you. It's a thank you. It'll go on the wall over there. I made it to fit that spot. Now you can have rhododendron flowers even in the wintertime!"

A slow smile spread over Windola's face and Rose smiled back, knowing the healer liked the idea.

"Here's more thread," Windola mentioned absently. She pulled a large assortment of thread and several small pieces of undyed material from her carrying bag.

Rose produced five embroideries of daisies over the next two weeks. She'd done that particular flower many times and didn't need the real thing in front of her. Windola took them with her when she went into town, and to Rose's rather obvious delight, Benk came back with her. She caught Windola smiling to herself.

"Benk's a friend," Rose explained when the young man went outside to water his horse.

Windola didn't answer. All she did was smile again. Rose bristled, but there wasn't much she could say to someone who wouldn't talk back. The young scout stayed for supper that night, and the cottage was filled with talk and laughter. The focal point of the evening came at the end as Benk was saying goodbye. He had teased Rose often about the Girls' Hut, laughing at the face she made every time he said the name. Standing at the door, he teased her one last time.

"Goodbye, Rose, and don't forget the Girls' Hut is waiting for you. Let me know when you're ready and I'll take you there."

She responded with her worst face of the evening.

"It will be good for you. You need to learn how to get along better with people. No more of that rude behavior I saw in Mount Pasture, please," he ordered in his most pompous style, quite as if he were Rose's father.

"You're not my father but—I'm ready. I'll go live in the Girls' Hut."

The stunned expression on Benk's face was quite satisfying, but Rose's enjoyment didn't last long.

Windola said, "I need to go too."

"What? Where are you going?" Rose asked indignantly, as

if she hadn't just agreed to her own departure.

The healer took a long breath to gather the words necessary to explain herself, but Benk took pity on her.

"Windola makes regular trips to gather plants she'll need over the winter. Most of the herbs for treating wintertime colds and fevers are more effective if they're as fresh as possible. She's probably delayed her trips to take care of you and needs to go as soon as possible."

"When should I leave?" Rose squeaked, unnerved at the sudden need for practicalities.

Benk put himself in charge, and the move was organized in three days.

There wasn't much for Rose to pack. She'd already donated the blankets, hammocks, and tree ladder to the scouts' supply room. Nurse Broomely's soft old scarf and the sachet with its embroidered puppy and goats were in the bottom of the backpack. Quickly Rose put what was left of her embroidery supplies on top of them. She didn't want to think about her past life—that would only add tears to tension. An old nightgown of Windola's went on top of the supplies and she was done.

The next day she found herself sitting on a horse again, following Benk out of the clearing. Her hands were clutching at the reins, and the only good thing she could think of was that the blue dress Janna had given her was still pretty, even though its color was faded from frequent washings.

I'll buy a new dress when my embroideries sell and I'm an independent craftswoman.

The thought lifted her spirits from flat-on-the-ground to right-beneath-her-horse's belly—but that was as high as they got. Benk seemed to know this was not a time to tease. Silently he slowed his horse so he could ride beside her. When they reached the borders of the village, she pulled on the reins nervously to stop her horse. The scout gazed at her, as if he were wondering how hard this day was going to be. Rose could see him out of the corner of an eye, but she didn't say anything.

I'm turning into another wordless Windola, but she couldn't have spoken without crying. In fact, it might be a good idea to close her eyes entirely. Oh well, as long as she had her eyes closed—Rose lifted her face and asked the Maker for help. Her request didn't take long. She darted a quick glance at Benk.

"That's it! If you're going to the Maker for help, you'll be fine," he said looking relieved. He waited a moment for her to respond. When she stayed quiet, he spoke up vigorously in support of his own words. "The worst part of any new thing is often the newness itself. Once that wears off, you'll be very happy."

"I hope so," she managed to say and they rode on.

The village they entered was the largest in Far Reaches, with several streets in its main section. The homes had small front yards but big back ones with gardens. *This isn't so bad*, Rose decided, but her hands were still clenched in a death grip on the reins. Benk turned at a street corner and led her past a row of shops that had no front yards at all. Instead they had windows that displayed whatever the shops sold.

"There," Benk said, pointing to a large window that was filled with handcrafts.

Rose saw two paintings that she didn't like very much. *Cottages aren't purple. And that bird is bigger than the tree it's perched on.* She liked the aprons and dresses displayed in one corner though. Bouquets of dried flowers filled the other corner, while expertly knitted shawls and sweaters took up a prominent place in the middle. There was no sign of her daisy embroideries, however, and she rode on beside Benk with her bottom lip poking out. If her embroideries weren't good enough to put in the shop window, how would they ever sell? How would she make a living?

They rode two blocks further. Then Benk stopped in front of a large wooden house with small windows. Rose knew it was the Girls' Hut before he swung off his horse. She sat without moving, getting used to the place. It was certainly bigger than the other homes. The yard in front was bigger too, though nothing much had been done to make it pretty. It needed more flowers. How could she live in a place with such small windows?

Finally she handed her reins to Benk who was beginning to shift from foot to foot. He helped her dismount and they entered the front door. A tall thin woman came from a side room to greet them.

"You'll be Rose," she said in a friendly enough manner.

Rose couldn't smile, even though she felt Benk's eyes upon her.

"I'm Leftie. It's not my real name, but since I hate my real name, I go by my nickname. I'm a left-handed knitter. That's how—"

Rose interrupted her. "Did you make those knitted things in the shop window?"

Leftie started at the abrupt question but responded readily enough. "Yes, they're mine. They'll sell better once the weather turns cool. Nobody wants to buy wool sweaters in the middle of summer."

"They are well done," Rose proclaimed.

A certain level of haughtiness had crept into her words. She noticed Benk wince at her side and tried again.

"I mean, they are quite beautiful. You are a very skillful knitter."

There, that had been better. Leftie was pleased and thanked her. Rose risked a glance at Benk. He gave her a look that approved and rebuked at the same time. She could almost hear him telling her to behave herself.

Two young women about Rose's age burst into the house.

"Benk, how nice to see you," they said with pleasure.

Benk greeted them warmly. There was no hidden rebuke on his face now. "Patrise, Melona, let me introduce you to Rose."

"You're our new roommate," the girls chorused.

Immediately Rose felt sick to her stomach. When Benk cleared his throat, she tried to rally.

"Hello. Why do you have to live here?"

The scout winced again, but the girls didn't seem to notice anything wrong with her word choice.

"Our parents died three years ago. We've been living in the Girls' Hut ever since. I teach in the school and Patrise paints for the craft shop," Melona explained cheerfully.

"Oh," Rose said. For the life of her, she couldn't think of anything else to say. *Those awful paintings!*

Benk filled what could have been an uncomfortable pause.

"Well ladies, I'll leave you now. Patrise, Melona, it was good to see you again. Leftie, let the scouts know if there are any odd jobs you need done around here. Rose, I'm sure you'll get settled soon and be very happy here."

Rose scowled at him and he made a hasty departure.

The other two girls chatted as they led her up the stairs to the room they shared. Rose followed, her stomach in knots. It was a large room. She was glad of that, but there was no getting around the fact that the three beds took up most of the space. There was very little privacy. Slowly Rose unpacked her embroidery threads and nightgown. She hesitated. Then she reached into the bottom of the backpack and pulled out the old blue scarf and sachet. She needed them.

"What's that?" asked Melona curiously.

"They belonged to my old nurse," Rose told her in a voice gone rusty.

"You embroidered this," guessed Patrise. She was peering intently at the sachet with its puppy and goats. "Was it one of your first things?"

"Yes."

Rose wished she hadn't unpacked her keepsakes. They were too personal.

"I have my first painting too. It's much worse than that sachet. I'd show it to you, but I think it's buried somewhere in the attic."

Rose thought of Patrise's purple cottages and glanced at her sachet with increased favor. She didn't say anything though. In fact she stayed quiet the rest of the day and lay in bed that night wondering if she could stand it. It was still dark outside when a bell rang early the next morning. Both her roommates groaned. Rose felt a brief spirit of comradery with them, enough to ask a question.

"Is breakfast always this early?"

"It is when Leftie cooks. She gets up in the middle of the night," Patrise grumbled.

Melona explained sleepily, "We take turns with the chores. My turn to cook comes on a non-school day, and we eat breakfast mid-morning!"

Rose smiled at her. It was her first smile in the Girls' Hut. When Melona smiled back, she felt as if she'd won a major victory.

During breakfast Leftie and the other morning people talked to each other. Rose ate in silence, but since several others were silent too, she didn't feel isolated. Patrise insisted on walking with her to the craft shop that morning.

"You can go on ahead. I know I'm slow," Rose said, wishing Patrise would leave her alone.

Patrise stayed right at her side, smiling with what Rose grudgingly admitted was genuine sympathy.

"I heard about your feet. I don't mind being leisurely. It feeds the imagination. We rush through life too much."

Rose didn't respond. A mental image of the larger-than-life bird had appeared in her mind. She doubted seriously that Patrise's imagination needed any feeding.

When they reached the shop, they found Leftie working at the front room desk. Around her were the crafts that were for sale. Rose studied them with such interest, Leftie came from behind the desk to give her a tour.

"Timbe makes the candles and he's a true artist. His straight candles taper perfectly without the slightest bend. He makes these fantastic shapes too, which are quite popular.

Warner makes tables, bookcases, cabinets—he's an amazing carpenter. Nobody even tries to compete with him. On the other hand, Sophie and Dita compete constantly over their whittling. It's a friendly competition—most of the time. Ming dries our flowers. They sell very well. Daniel makes the metal gates and fastenings. You won't see him much. He has a workshop behind his home. Warner, Timbe, and both whittlers do too, for that matter.

"You'll be joining Patrise and me in the back room. She paints in one corner and I knit in a chair by the fire. You can choose whatever other part of the room you want for your embroidery work. Ming comes in occasionally, but she's sporadic with her flowers, and we don't give her any special place. Four children and a husband take up most of Ming's time."

Rose critiqued the various crafts as Leftie pointed to them. There were two end tables and a bookcase in the front room. She agreed that they were exceptionally well made, and she liked the candles, especially the straight ones. There was something beautiful about their perfect symmetry. The fantastically shaped ones didn't appeal to her nearly as much. They weren't like anything from real life. *At least they aren't pretending to be,* she decided, averting her eyes from another painting of birds nesting in a tree much too small for them. It was similar to the painting in the window, though these birds were orange with bright blue swirls on their wings.

"Each of us is assigned a day to sit in the front room and take care of customers," Leftie continued. "Yours won't come until you've had time to settle in. I'll stay with you the first time and show you how. Come on back and see our supplies."

In no time Rose found herself sitting in a comfortable chair contemplating a large piece of clean cloth. Her eyebrows lowered and her lips pressed tightly together.

"Having trouble with inspiration?" Patrise asked.

"No."

Rose never lacked ideas for her embroideries. That

was not what was bothering her. Her daisy pictures were bothering her—or the lack of them. They weren't in the front of the shop or in the back room where they must have been framed. What had these people done with them? She glared over at the rocking chair where Leftie was knitting so quickly that her long needles were a blur.

"Where are my daisies?" she asked darkly.

If these people didn't like her embroidery, she'd leave; that's what she'd do.

Leftie laughed and Rose stiffened. She would not tolerate being laughed at; she would move to a place that—

"They sold before we could frame them. They weren't even out of the back room. People have been clamoring for more. You do exquisite work, Rose!"

Rose's face flushed with pleasure. Not many compliments had come her way in Yospaldo. She looked at the fabric in her hand again and irises took shape, purple irises against a background of tall grass.

The rest of the morning was without incident. The thread drawer didn't contain enough colored threads to suit Rose, and she made a tutting noise with her mouth in a perfect imitation of Nurse Broomely. The thought of her old nurse gave her a pang of sadness; however, the threads quickly claimed her concentration again. She would have to dye more colors, lots more colors, and this time she wouldn't need to rely on Windola to find everything she needed.

Blackberries. It was the right time of year for them and they produced a rich purple. The bark from a sweetgum tree would work too. Its dye would be darker than she wanted, but a touch of it here or there would give the flowers depth.

There were green threads already in the shop, but they were rejected as totally unsatisfactory. Rose would have thrown them away if she hadn't known that she could dye them over again. She was certain she'd seen spinach leaves in the Girls' Hut garden. They'd make a beautiful green, as would lilac flowers if she could find them. Oh, and gardens usually had peppermint plants. Peppermint leaves made a dark khaki green, which wasn't really what she wanted, but she could work it in for contrast.

The craft shop had plenty of salt and vinegar to set her colors. She could see plainly marked boxes of both items in a corner of the room. Leftie must use them for her yarn. *Salt for berry dyes; vinegar for plant dyes.* Without warning, her mind flew backwards in time. Nurse Broomely had told the five-year-old Rose that she was adding a half-cup salt to 8 cups of water in order to make her dye fast.

Rose had asked, "Is the dye slow now?"

Her nurse had tried to explain. "When my material simmers for an hour in the salt water, then the dye I add later on will set in the fabric and not run the first time I wash it."

The little girl had said wisely, "The dye may be fast, but the salt is faster, right?"

Nurse Broomely had told Rose that story so many times over the years that she'd never been sure whether she remembered the actual event or just the telling.

Leftie reached for her bag of yarn and knocked a knitting needle off the table. It clattered onto the floor, startling Rose out of her memories. *Good memories. Not everything in my past was bad.*

Threading a needle with brown thread from the drawer, Rose settled in her chair. She'd show a little bit of ground here and a fallen twig there.

When it was lunchtime, Leftie produced a basket of food for the three of them, and they went into the craft shop's back yard. At first Rose and Patrise were still absorbed by their work and munched without speaking. Leftie eyed them with amusement.

"FLOWERS!" Rose exclaimed out of nowhere.

"What?" asked both Patrise and Leftie, who were understandably startled.

"This yard needs flowers. How have you people worked here day after day without flowers?"

"You're right. Flowers would be uplifting," Patrise agreed.

"NeitherPatrise nor I are gardeners," Leftie dryly pointed out.

"I can plant them. I'll search for seeds when I leave this afternoon," Rose argued heatedly. She expected Leftie to refuse permission, but the older woman surprised her.

"Seeds won't be any problem. Anyone in town would be happy to share them with us. If you'll do the gardening, I'll get the seeds."

Rose tried to relax her body. Nobody had rebuked her. Nobody had laughed at her.

"Where are you going this afternoon?" Patrise asked. "Your feet—"

She paused eloquently, and Rose made an impatient motion with her hand.

"I need plants for dye and I'm through babying my feet. Is there a basket I can take?"

Leftie found her an old basket easily enough. As soon as she had it in her hands, Rose charged out the door, desperate to be by herself. Ruthlessly she plundered the Girls' Hut garden for spinach and peppermint leaves. A sweetgum tree was growing in the next-door neighbor's yard. It only took her a few minutes, to strip all the bark she needed. Blackberries were a problem though. There weren't any in sight. She wandered down the road away from town, ready to take what she needed wherever she found it, and it was perhaps fortunate for the neighboring gardeners, who might have wanted to keep what they'd grown, that she found a wild blackberry patch in a sunny spot.

She was filling her basket with the berries when someone spoke right behind her.

"I wouldn't make a pie with those. The wild ones are usually too tart."

Chapter 10

SUMMER

Rose jumped and then whipped around to find a young man with black wavy hair and dark eyes smiling at her. He sat on a nearby rock as if he intended to stay.

She stared at him coldly. His features were handsome; his muscles developed; worst of all, his moustache was thick. Most of the Yospaldon lords had thick moustaches. They were very proud of them. Frowning as she went back to her berries, she hoped the horrid young man would leave. He didn't.

"My name is Dalc."

She kept on picking berries.

"My family owns one of the few farms in Far Reaches. The woods are constantly trying to take over the fields, but we like farming and it's a service to the people here."

"Farming is good," Rose condescended to say. She was trying hard to keep her temper. She wasn't in Yospaldo; she was in Far Reaches. This young man was not a Yospaldon.

"What are you going to make with those berries?"

"Purple dye."

"That's fine then. Why don't I hold the basket while you pick?"

"No."

Maybe he would go away if she ignored him. It didn't happen, of course. She knew this type of man. Probably all the girls in Far Reaches received his attentions breathlessly. Her indifference would be intriguing to him.

"Where do you live?"

"The Girls' Hut."

"When you've finished picking your berries, I'll buy you a sweet at the bakery. Then I can walk you home."

Rose was fed up with this young man. "I've got a better idea. Why don't you go back to your farm and soak your face in—"

"Wait up, Rose," someone called at that opportune moment, and Melona rushed up to them. "Hi, Dalc," she said shyly.

Dalc nodded at her. Melona was overweight and her nose was big. Rose guessed that he had never asked Melona to have a sweet with him, though there was no doubt but that her answer would have been different from Rose's. She was staring at Dalc as if he were the most wonderful thing in Montaland. Rose had seen that look before. *Poor girl!*

"Hi Melona, is school over for the day?" she greeted her roommate much more warmly than she would have if they had been alone.

As she spoke, Rose put a hand on Melona's arm and steered her back toward town. Behind them she could hear Dalc laugh softly.

"He likes you. Dalc likes you!" Melona whispered.

"Too bad, I don't like him," Rose said crushingly.

Melona's eyes widened but she didn't say anything. Rose couldn't think of anything to say either, so the two girls walked silently to the craft shop, where one started preparing her dyes while the other admired her sister's new painting.

It took the rest of the afternoon for Rose to crush the spinach and peppermint leaves, cut the sweet gum bark into small pieces, and smash the blackberries. As she finished each one, she stirred it into a container of hot water. Threads would sit in them overnight, slowly changing to rich dark colors.

Tomorrow she would hang those threads to dry. Then she'd pour the dyed water from the four big containers into small ones, adding water of differing amounts to each color so that she'd wind up with a range of lighter hues. Finally she'd heat the water in each of the smaller containers and soak threads in them.

When there was nothing left to do that day, Rose went hesitantly over to join the two sisters. Melona was working on her lesson plans. Patrise was standing in front of her easel, dabbing bright pink onto the new painting. Rose stared at it in shock. *It looks like a spill someone stepped in and smeared.*

Melona asked excitedly, "Isn't it beautiful?"

"I don't know. I can't tell what it is," Rose answered awkwardly.

"It's a sunset I saw the other night," Patrise told her, picking up another brush so she could swirl orange in the middle of the two biggest pink dabs.

Rose continued to stare hard at the painting. She lived with these girls. It would be better not to offend them.

"Well, it's got the sunset colors but where's the sky? Are there clouds that I'm not seeing?" she asked and was pleased with her tact, especially since she was not in the habit of exercising any.

Patrise stuck her brushes in a jar of water and started to wash her hands. "I don't want clouds. They'd detract from the vividness of the colors."

"But isn't it clouds that absorb the light and become sunset colors?"Rose asked feeling confused.

"I don't want it to look like a real sunset. It's my impression of the sunset that counts, not what it's really like. When I saw it in the sky the other night, it overwhelmed me with its intensity. I wanted to show that in my picture."

Rose, who diligently studied flowers in order to embroider them as realistically as possible, was shaking her head.

"That would be like me making a daisy embroidery out of swirls. It wouldn't be as pretty as the real flower."

"I think it would be. You should do it," suggested Patrise with considerable interest.

While Rose shuddered at the thought, Melona put an arm around each of their shoulders and drew them out of the shop, obviously hoping to end the conversation. It didn't work. The two young women argued over art every step of the way to the Girls' Hut, but what was encouraging to Rose was that she didn't lose her temper. Patrise was passionately defending inferior art, and Rose didn't lose her temper.

I'm improving!

Over the next three weeks, there were all too many opportunities to improve. Sometimes Rose kept back the scathing words; sometimes she didn't. Neither Patrise nor Melona ever seemed to get angry, which was hard to understand considering how provoking Rose knew she was at times. It was undeniably impressive.

In their turn, Patrise and Melona were impressed by Rose's easy conquest of every young man in the village and surrounding area.

"It's not as if you flirt with them. You aren't even nice to them," Melona said one afternoon.

"You snub every last one of them," agreed Patrise from the window where she was hanging socks to dry.

Both girls stared speculatively at their new roommate who was lying on top of her bedspread, too tired to take her shoes off.

"Young men are stupid," was the new roommate's addition to the conversation.

"Even Benk?" asked Patrise slyly.

"He is better than most, but he has his moments."

"I wish I was as pretty as you," Melona admitted wistfully.

Rose sat straight up and stared at her.

"Are you crazy? You're much prettier than I am. Patrise is too!"

The two sisters looked at each other. "It's the fumes from her dyes. They've affected her brain," Patrise solemnly informed her sister.

There was moisture in Melona's eyes. Was she crying?

"Listen to me because I'm only going to say this once," Rose ordered, borrowing a no-nonsense quote from Nurse Broomely. "It's not the outside of a person that's important. There are plenty of attractive outsides at Yospaldo but trust me, those women aren't beautiful. They aren't even pretty."

"Yeah yeah," Patrise said with an air of long-suffering patience. "We've heard that all our lives. It's what's inside a person that matters. That's what people say to plain girls."

Rose's face flamed. She could tell because of how hot she suddenly felt, but at that point she didn't care if steam was coming from her ears.

"They're right. The people who say that are right. It's the inside that makes a person pretty. You'd be disgusted if you picked an apple with a smooth red skin and cut it open to find rot inside. That's the way I am."

"Rose," said Melona gently, but Rose wasn't finished.

"I lost my temper this afternoon with Leftie. There is nobody kinder than Leftie, and I yelled at her because she'd moved my light purple threads to a different place. She apologized, but I discovered later that she'd moved the threads because they were getting splashed with water whenever people washed their hands at the sink. I was so upset that I yelled at her again for not telling me."

Rose began to shake.

"Don't tell me I should pay attention to those stupid young men. They don't have any sense. If they did, they'd leave me alone and concentrate on you two."

"Rose!" Patrise said firmly, putting a stop to Rose's outburst with the one word.

Patrise was much more authoritative than Melona when she was aroused.

She'd make a better school teacher than Melona, Rose couldn't help but think. *There'd be no discipline problems with Patrise at the head of a classroom, while Melona could undoubtedly paint much, much—*

"You're wrong about us. We do things wrong too, but the Maker loves us anyway."

"Yeah yeah. That's what people say to rotten apples," Rose muttered.

"That means every one of us," Patrise stated decisively. "It's why the Maker died in the old world. He took everyone's rottenness on himself. If we want to be included, we're forgiven! And loved!"

There was quiet in the room as Rose took a long shuddering breath. The expression on Patrise's face was so quelling that a bee on the window sill quit buzzing and slipped stealthily out of the room.

Melona couldn't take the heavy atmosphere.

"Besides, you couldn't be a smooth red apple, Rose. That's an awful metaphor. You don't have red hair," she pointed out and smiled with satisfaction when the other two started laughing.

Rose felt almost fond of her roommates after that, which didn't prevent her from exploding with anger a few days later. It was Benk's fault. He had stopped to visit early one evening and quickly accepted their supper invitation. Everything was following the normal pattern until Leftie commented on how long he'd been in Far Reaches.

"It's been over a month. That's a record!"

"I've been taking a well-deserved break," Benk said, reaching for another biscuit.

"Are you leaving soon?" Melona asked.

"It depends. I'm waiting to hear something."

Swiftly he cut the hot biscuit open, slid a thick wedge of softened butter onto the bottom followed by a heaping spoonful of blackberry jam, smashed the top back on, and ate the whole thing without losing a drop of butter or jam. The women watched the whole procedure with awe.

"What are you waiting to hear?" was the next question.

"Scout stuff. What's for dessert?"

"It doesn't have anything to do with Yospaldo, does it?"

Rose asked darkly.

Benk shrugged. "We have our fingers in a lot of pies. Funny, that brings me back to my question—what's for dessert?"

"Blueberry pie," Patrise answered, as Rose took a bite of meat. "The last few weeks, you've stopped in whenever we have blueberry pie. It never fails."

Benk stared at her, a hurt expression on his face. "I don't know what you're talking about. My informants let me know when you're having cake and ice cream too. By the way, you haven't made any ice cream, have you? It's good on blueberry pie."

Patrise continued, ignoring his question and tapping her chin as if in deep thought. "If it's not Leftie's blueberry pie, it must be something else. Now let me see. What's changed in the Girls' Hut? Oh yes—that would be Rose."

Rose choked on her bite of meat.

"Don't start, Patrise," she sputtered and meant it. She could take Patrise's teasing about Benk in private, but not around other people and certainly not around Benk himself.

"Wel-l-l," drawled Benk. "That would be true."

Rose choked on the gulp of water she had taken to help her swallow the meat.

Benk gazed soulfully at her. "I needed to check up on this girl. Make sure she was behaving herself."

"All right, that's enough. Give Rose a chance to swallow," Leftie rebuked the table-at-large.

The table-at-large gave Rose time to swallow and then promptly started up again.

"I told her not to be snooty, you see," Benk said.

"Rose isn't snooty," Melona defended her roommate.

"Yes, I am," Rose disagreed, watching Benk out of the sides of her eyes. His hand stopped halfway to his mouth, and the forkful of food it was holding hung in midair. Yes! She had surprised him again.

"Occasionally maybe, but it doesn't matter. Benk warned

us you might be," Melona said soothingly.

"HE WHAT?"

Patrise tried to fix things.

"No big deal, Rose. He said you didn't know how to get along with people because of where you grew up, and for us to be patient."

Rose exploded. The women she was getting used to, the women she had even begun to like, became untrustworthy strangers again.

"You talked about me to these Girls' Hut people. How dare you! You had no right!" she shouted furiously.

Patrise looked stricken; Melona had tears rolling down her cheeks; everyone else was staring at her with hurt eyes.

There were other angry words rushing up her throat, words that would hurt them even more. Rose pushed her chair back so hard it fell to the floor. Then she ran through the house to the front door. She had every intention of running until she was far, far away, but one of her feet caught on the doorstep and twisted. Great. Now she had a broken ankle. It hurt to walk, but Rose gritted her teeth and made it to the back yard. At least people passing by on the road couldn't see her there.

She sat behind a bush and bent her face to her knees. The minutes passed and her anger did too. She didn't even know why she had gotten angry. *Pride.* The voice was kind but unyielding, and Rose started crying.

Someone patted her awkwardly on the back. That wasn't the Maker. The Maker wasn't awkward.

"I'm fine," she muttered.

"Of course you are. That would be why you're hiding behind a bush."

Rose sat up and sniffed, prompting Benk to dig in his pocket and hand her a handkerchief. She wiped her eyes and cheeks.

"It's only been used a few times."

When she dropped the handkerchief and tried to clean her hands on the grass, Benk grinned. "I'm kidding. It's clean."

She didn't grin back; neither did she frown. She was too miserable to react.

"One day at a time, Rose."

"Do you think they'll let me stay?"

"They will. I told them to," he announced in full pompous style.

Rose rolled her eyes, but she let him help her up and didn't even object when he supported her across the yard and into the sitting room. Her housemates made a fuss over her ankle and settled her on the sofa with a cushion under her foot.

"I'm sorry," she apologized to everybody except Benk, who was really too cocky for his own good.

Nobody noticed the omission but Benk, who just grinned again.

Rose's ankle was sprained, not broken. She had to embroider on the Girls' Hut sofa while she put cold packs on the swelling, but that only lasted a few days. It was a relief to leave the house and hobble back to work, but she found a new problem at the shop. Her finished embroideries were selling as soon as Leftie displayed them in the window, and people insisted on walking down the hall to the workroom to see her current project. Rose didn't like anyone inspecting something she was working on. She glared at the potential customers, but they were undaunted and always bought the embroidery on the spot. Finishing it in a huff, she'd start another only to have the same thing happen.

Her temper might have flared again if Leftie and Patrise hadn't agreed with her. They made up a new rule, and Leftie made sure it was enforced.

"No more customers in the back room. No more," she informed the shopkeeper every morning, leaning forward to emphasize her point. "There have been too many interruptions, and we need to catch up on our work."

A few of the shopkeepers mentioned pointedly that needing to catch up on their work didn't stop the back room from taking frequent breaks, but all such comments were roundly ignored.

"I liked your embroidery of white, climbing roses the best. They looked so real, I kept leaning over to smell them," Leftie told Rose one morning from her rocking chair.

"I like the daisies best," Melona said from a corner. It was a holiday at school, and she was doing lesson plans in the room with them.

"Which color?" asked Rose who was secretly plotting to give one of her embroideries to the Girls' Hut. That kitchen needed brightening. A daisy embroidery would be cheerful, and it wouldn't take long to do.

In between her larger projects, Rose dashed off daisies of all sizes and colors. They were relaxing to make because she could do them without thinking. It was an added bonus that they came in several different colors. She never felt as if she was repeating the same flower.

Melona laughed. "I can never choose. Whatever you're working on is my favorite—until I see the next one!"

"I have a request if you're thinking of the embroidery you're planning to give the Girls' Hut," Patrise said, smirking at the start of surprise Rose made.

Rose smirked right back at her. "Oh-h-h, have you decided that pictures of real things are the best?"

"Certainly not! I want that embroidery covered with swirls you promised to make. It could be called 'Essence of a Daisy.'"

"I never promised to make such a thing. It's a terrible idea," Rose disagreed heatedly, and the two of them were off again.

Leftie and Melona glanced at each other. Melona rolled

her eyes, and Leftie was about to do the same thing when the brilliant idea of announcing an early lunch came to her. The weather was comfortably warm still, but summer was waning on the high mountain. There wouldn't be many more days of picnic weather. For a few minutes, sandwiches took precedence over art. Afterwards Melona left to do an errand, while everyone else went inside to work. Rose sat in her chair, but she was feeling restless. Putting her embroidery down, she stretched.

"I need a walk," she said just as they heard the door to the shop open.

The sound of people talking was distant at first. When it got louder, everyone in the back room tensed. Ming was keeping the shop that day, and she was bringing a customer down the hall even though it was against the new rule.

Rose scowled and hid her embroidery under the cushion of her chair.

"It'll get smashed," Leftie warned.

"I don't care. No one is seeing any more of my unfinished work," Rose insisted.

She stood in front of her chair as the door opened, but her defensive stance was broken when a woman with a beaming face walked into the room.

"Janna!" everyone exclaimed.

Everyone knew Janna. Everyone liked Janna, and they had all been friends with her for years. Rose had listened to them talk about how funny Janna had behaved when she was pregnant or how helpful she'd been doing this or how understanding she'd been doing that. Jealousy had loomed, but Rose had controlled it without much problem while Janna was gone on her camping trip.

That trip was now over—as was Rose's control. Jealousy shot down roots and grew to a towering height within seconds. Patrise and Leftie hopped up to welcome their friend, but Rose got there first. Fiercely she hugged the older woman.

I will be Janna's best friend! I will be.

Janna greeted everyone and then turned to Rose.

"I hear you've been doing beautiful work."

"Thanks. Let me show you—"

Patrise interrupted with mischief in her eyes. "I do wish we could show you what she's working on, but Rose doesn't like people to see her embroideries unfinished. I'm very sorry. Would you like to see my meadow?"

"No, she doesn't," Rose snapped. "It's not a meadow anyway; it's a senseless hodgepodge of green slashes and red dots."

There was silence in the room. Rose pulled her embroidery out from under the cushion and turned around to see everyone staring at her, everyone but Patrise. Patrise was bending over her picture, but she wasn't painting.

Janna recovered first.

"I would like to see them both, of course, and I would like to see that sweater Leftie is knitting too. It's my favorite color, deep blue like the late evening sky."

Slowly Rose let the hand holding her embroidery drop down by her side. *What have I done?*

The problem was she was still jealous. She wanted Janna to look at her embroidery and not pay any attention to Patrise's work. At that moment she was even jealous of Leftie. She didn't want to be, but she was. Rose closed her eyes.

MAKE me do right.

Hesitantly she walked over to Patrise.

"I'm sorry," she whispered.

When Patrise straightened up and wiped an eye, Rose could have died. She had made Patrise cry—Patrise who was kind and patient; Patrise who argued endlessly in support of her beloved paintings.

Rose moved in front of the picture of the meadow.

"You know, it's really pretty in its own way. I mean, the colors are wonderful and if you use your imagination heavily, it does look like a meadow!"

Patrise smiled.

"From you, that's a supreme compliment," she managed to say, but her words were shaky.

Rose stayed in front of the picture. She couldn't step away from it. Her body and nerves tightened to an unbearable tautness. She belonged back in Yospaldo; that was where she belonged, with all the other awful people.

"Patrise, I would rather die than hurt you," she croaked right before an enormous burp burst from her mouth.

"There'll be hiccups next," she warned, and right after she said the words, the first one arrived.

The room sprang into action.

"Lift your left arm above your head," Leftie called, bustling over.

"Hold your breath as long as you can," Patrise advised, hovering close.

"Drink water in little sips while you're holding your breath," Janna ordered, going for a glass of water.

HIC.

Rose raised her left arm and held her breath.

HIC.

"Little sips," Janna reminded her as she arrived with the glass of water.

Taking a deep breath and holding it, Rose took little sips of water. She counted to eleven.

HIC.

She started over again and got to thirteen.

HIC.

"Run outside and jog around town. It'll change your breathing pattern," Patrise yelled.

Rose got a mental image of herself dashing across the village's main street, every other step punctuated by a loud hiccup. She started laughing and her breathing pattern sped up.

"I can't— HIC—do that— HIC —my feet— HIC —and—

HIC —I'd look— HIC —crazy."

"Who cares?" Patrise yelled even louder. "At least it would get rid of those pesky young men who follow you everywhere."

HIC.

Everyone was laughing now. Rose felt her way through the room, tears of laughter almost blinding her. She needed to sit down.

"BOO!"

Ming had jumped from behind the door and yelled right in Rose's face. The girl flinched away into Janna who bumped into Leftie who started to fall. Patrise caught at the three of them, only to lose her balance and crash down too.

"Are you trying to scare us out of our wits, Ming?" Leftie asked severely from where she lay. She wasn't trying to move yet. She had to check first and see if her arms and legs were working. She was too old to fall.

"Janna, we're so glad you dropped in!" Patrise screamed hysterically into Janna's ear, which had wound up on the floor right next to Patrise's face.

While Patrise and Rose rolled about with laughter, Janna managed to get to her feet and help Leftie up. They sat down heavily in chairs. Then they laughed. It was good to laugh at life, but it was wise to do it from the security of a sturdy chair.

Ming wasn't sorry for anything. In fact, she had an undeniably smug expression on her face. Leftie felt that a light word of reprimand was in order.

"You mustn't try to frighten people!" she scolded with what she felt was the right mixture of gentleness and firmness.

"Oh yeah," the unrepentant Ming said. "There's nothing like a good scare to get rid of the hiccups!"

It was true. Rose's hiccups were gone. She and Patrise hopped up from the floor and stood grinning.

"Happy to oblige, Rose," Ming remarked airily, walking

back through the hall to the shop.

"Anyone want to go for a walk?" Rose asked.

Everyone stared at her.

"Maybe next time," Patrise said giggling.

Leftie shook her head. She was going to sit in her rocking chair for at least an hour. Then she was going back to the Girls' Hut and soak in a hot bath.

"Not now, Rose, but come for supper tomorrow night," Janna found breath to say.

"I'd love to," Rose told her with pleasure and left the room. They heard her thanking Ming in the front of the shop as she left.

Patrise giggled at Ming's self-satisfied answer.

Janna took a deep breath. "I think I'll go home. Leftie, are you all right?"

Patrise giggled at the question.

"Help me to the Girls' Hut and I will be," Leftie answered, changing her plans. She didn't want to be left in the room with a chronic giggler.

Patrise could read her friend's face perfectly well. She dissolved into a helpless fit of giggles. The two older women made their way carefully out of the room. Patrise giggled for a few minutes by herself, unable to stop. Finally she went to the sink and doused her face with cold water. There, that had helped. She had stopped giggling.

She turned composedly around and saw her meadow picture on its easel. Rose's embroidery was on the floor in front of it—realism kneeling to impressionism. Oh no!

A fresh, seemingly inexhaustible stream of giggles poured from Patrise's mouth. Rescuing the embroidery from the floor, she put it on Rose's chair and went into the back yard. She would lie flat on her back in the summer grass and gaze into the sky. That would be inspiring.

Inspiration faded into sleep, and Patrise was finally cured of the giggles.

Chapter 11

Fall

"What did your group decide to do?" Petten asked Benk.

The older scout had waited until Rose was in the middle of telling Janna something that had happened in the craft shop, and even then he spoke in an undertone. Benk replied in a low whisper.

Neither man took into account the level of devotion involved in hero worship.

"I can't hear what Benk's saying," complained Largen loudly.

"Me neither. What's your group going to do?" asked Tuff.

Rose quit talking in the middle of a sentence and stared at Benk through narrowed eyes. He'd been invited to all four of the meals she'd shared with Janna and Petten's family over the last three weeks. She wouldn't have seen very much of him otherwise. Whenever she'd asked what he was doing, he had told her it was scouting work and to mind her own business. The only thing she knew was that he'd been training a young mare called Dandy, named after her mincing prance.

Earlier that evening as they rode to Janna's cabin, Benk had bragged about how quickly Dandy had finished her training. Rose had narrowed her eyes then too. She knew he'd spent over a year training his first horse, Follower. There had to be a reason why he wasn't doing the same thing now, but she'd mustered all her will-power and stayed silent. An argument would have spoiled their ride.

"Benk's group decided to eat more and talk less," Petten answered Tuff's question now.

"Good idea," chorused the boys and proceeded to put the plan into action.

Rose wasn't that easily distracted, and she didn't even think about mustering will-power.

"Don't," she told Benk and Petten.

"Don't eat more or don't talk less?" Benk asked.

"You know what I mean. The scouts are sticking their noses where they shouldn't. They need to forget Yospaldo."

"Yes, ma'am. Sorry. I forgot you're the boss of the scouts."

Nine-year-old Alissa decided to interrupt this boring conversation.

"Benk, who are you taking to the Fall Festival this year?"

"Oh-h, I don't know," Benk drawled, while Rose's face took on a long-suffering expression.

The winters were notoriously bad in Far Reaches, with blizzards and high winds that could blow a person off his or her feet, in which case it was unfortunate if there was a cliff nearby. A network of caves inside the mountain was the kingdom's answer. Some of the caves were natural and others laboriously made, but they provided a warm, safe refuge during the winter months.

Far Reaches was one of the highest kingdoms in Montaland, but it wasn't one of the largest. Not only were all its inhabitants able to bunch up inside the mountain, they were also able to get together twice a year, once in the fall and once in the spring. The festivals were events everyone looked forward to—everyone but Rose.

Melona had been talking non-stop about the Fall Festival ever since cooler weather had arrived. Patrise was every bit as interested in it. Even Leftie was eager for the good time and speculated endlessly over the weather on the chosen day. Rose had been glad to get away from the three of them for the evening, but now Janna's family was just as bad.

"Wipe that expression off your face. You'll love our Fall Festival. It's a wonderful event," Janna told her briskly.

"There's singing and music," little Iris said.

"And lots of good food," added Largen, rubbing his stomach.

"Yeah," Tuff agreed with his older brother, rubbing his stomach exactly where Largen had rubbed his.

Janna laughed. "The boys like it because there are too many people around for me to keep track of what they eat. They can have as many desserts as they want."

"Yeah," Tuff said again, giving himself away. Largen poked him.

Benk picked up his glass and then paused, as if remembering something. "I know who's taking Rose to the Festival. Dalc has spread the word. He's going to hound your every step until you decide to go with him."

He nodded at the enraged girl across the table.

"I refuse to go with him," Rose sputtered. Then she groaned. "He'll pester me. I know he will."

"That's the plan," the scout agreed.

Rose leaned toward him in desperation. "You've got to take me, Benk. I can't think of any other way to get rid of Dalc. If he knows you've invited me, he'll leave me alone."

Benk rubbed his chin. "Dalc is a little stuck on himself. It might be good for his character development. Okay, I'll take you."

Rose sank back into her chair, closing her eyes in relief. She missed the wink Benk gave Janna.

The next day Rose lost no time in letting people know that she was going to the festival with Benk. She wanted Dalc to hear so he wouldn't pester her. It seemed to work. The young farmer was friendly but not a problem, not like Melona and Patrise who stared at her with knowing eyes until Rose rudely told them to stop.

"Who's taking you?" she asked in an effort to make up for her rudeness.

Melona sighed. "I'll go with Bosky again. He always asks me and I always go with him. He's not very exciting."

She finished with another sigh but Rose wasn't taking that.

"Bosky is one of the nicest young men in Far Reaches and he has good sense too. That's why he's in love with you."

"He's pudgy," Melona objected half-heartedly.

"Of course he's pudgy. He's a baker. Bakers have to be pudgy. It's the law," Patrise solemnly informed her sister.

"But if we got married, we'd both be pudgy and that would be embarrassing," wailed Melona.

"Nonsense. Do I have to go into the rotten apple metaphor again?" threatened Rose.

"No!"

"Spare us!"

Rose smiled with satisfaction. She had finally gotten through to them.

"Who's taking you," she asked Patrise.

Patrise shrugged. "I haven't been asked so far, but someone will once the prettier girls have been snapped up."

"I am holding a bright red apple," Rose said sternly, holding out an empty hand. "It looks pretty on the outside but—"

She stopped.

It is hard to continue an instructive metaphor when two pillows have hit you in the face.

―――――※―――――

Leftie predicted rain, but the morning of the festival dawned clear and bright, though there was a sharp bite to the air. Cold weather was coming. The inhabitants of Far Reaches needed to winterize their homes, pack, and move—but not today. Today was set aside to celebrate fall.

Rose and Patrise went to the craft shop in the morning as usual. Both of them were too involved in their latest projects to take the whole day off. Rose was embroidering the red and yellow zinnias she had planted in the shop's back yard. The colors were cheerful, and she wanted to put them on her bedroom wall that winter after she was buried alive inside a mountain.

She wasn't happy about living in a cave.

Patrise was working on a painting that featured giant swirls of gray with touches of blue. Rose hadn't asked what it was supposed to be; nor did she want to admit that she kind of liked it. If she could think of the painting as thick gray mist on a blue lake, it would be better for all concerned. Knowing Patrise, it was an impression of the gray cat with blue eyes that lived at the Girls' Hut.

Mid-morning Leftie arrived with a triumphant expression on her face.

"It's raining!"

Rose and Patrise rushed to the nearest window. Sure enough, clouds had come out of nowhere to cover the sky. A gentle rain was falling. Fortunately the rain stopped in half an hour and the sun shone again.

"There'll be several hours of sunshine to dry the grass so people can sit on it without getting wet," Leftie said in a virtuous tone of voice, as if she had ordered it that way, and the girls hid smiles. Since her predicted rain had arrived, Leftie could be happy with the sunshine. Otherwise she would have fussed the rest of the day over why it hadn't rained.

That afternoon Benk rode Dandy to the Girls' Hut with Firefly following. Firefly was an older bay mare with a relaxed manner that Rose liked, though her dull red coat wasn't nearly as attractive as Dandy's glossy black. They walked the horses through the woods to the large pasture used for the Fall Festival.

"What do you want to do first?" Benk asked after they had put the mares into an adjoining pasture.

"I don't know," Rose said, breathing in short gasps.

The large pasture was crowded. There were tents in one corner with people waiting their turn to play darts, ball games, balance competitions, and other types of amusements. Musicians played in the opposite corner, and people either danced or sprawled on the grass listening to them. The biggest group though was milling around the food tables in the middle of the pasture. Rose caught a glimpse of Largen and Tuff with loaded plates before they darted under a man's elbow.

This will be different from Yospaldon parties.

Her self-talk didn't work. She felt tight all over. Even her tongue was pressed against the roof of her mouth. Crowds still meant danger to her. Her mind was telling her body to relax, but her body was not obeying.

I've got to relax! If I don't, I'll start burping! Or get the hiccups!

"Are you hungry?" asked Benk.

"No."

She was too tense to be hungry. The last time she'd felt this way, she'd burped loudly and then got the hiccups. Both.

"Then let's go listen to the musicians for a while."

Rose was glad when they sat on a rock toward the back of the listeners. Closing her eyes, she let the music soothe her. When her eyes opened again, she found herself looking at a golden tree standing on a little knoll outside the pasture. Its leaves glowed in the late afternoon sunshine.

I should embroider a tree.

Benk shifted positions and Rose glanced at him. He smiled.

"Feeling better?"

"Could you tell?" she asked with embarrassment.

"Yes. I know groups of people are not your favorite thing."

"I think I'll be okay now. The music has helped."

"Great! Then let's get something to eat," Benk said, hopping to his feet.

Rose made a comment about men never growing up

when it came to food. Benk argued vigorously that food was a good thing, given to human beings by the Maker and meant to be enjoyed. Rose laughed loudly. By that time they had reached the food tables. Benk loaded his plate as if to prove his point, but Rose only got bread, a little chicken, and some grapes--food that would be easy on a nervous stomach. They made their way out of the crowd and joined Janna, Petten, and their children on a large blanket.

As she ate, Rose started to feel very happy. She was handling this crowd of people. She was even beginning to feel a comfortable sense of belonging in Far Reaches. The kingdom and the people who lived in it were becoming her kingdom and her people.

The rest of the evening passed in a pleasant blur. Benk and Rose listened to more music, watched the people who were folk dancing, played a few of the simple throwing games, and snubbed Dalc whenever they ran into him. He totally ignored the two of them, but they snubbed him anyway. Benk was as bad as Rose.

They rode home under a starry sky.

"I wonder how the Maker thought of stars," Rose said, staring up at them. Benk made no comment and she continued. "I think he's the greatest artist of all, but he makes things that look real—none of this impressions type stuff."

When Benk remained silent, Rose glanced over at him. He wasn't looking at the stars; he was looking at her. Rose turned away.

"Don't you think so, Benk?" she asked to break the silence.

"Yeah, he's an artist."

"A whole sky of little lights," Rose murmured helpfully.

Benk refused to be managed. "I'm leaving soon."

Rose jumped though she'd known this was coming.

"Where are you going?"

When Benk didn't answer, she pounded the front of her saddle. "The scouts should leave Yospaldo alone, do you hear me! It's bad. You have a good kingdom here. You should stay in it and forget places like Yospaldo."

"And the Maker's people who live there—we should forget them too?" Benk asked.

Rose started to say, "Yes," but the word wouldn't come. She hadn't forgotten Ricaldo's broad back and smile. How had he fared after helping her escape?

"What are you going to do?" she asked when they reached the Girls' Hut. There was a tremor in her words that she couldn't control, so she busied herself with getting off her horse.

One leg had to come around. That was fairly easy by now, but then came the hard part—sliding down Firefly's side. Dismounting by herself was a new accomplishment she was proud of, though the final thump onto the ground made her feet twinge. She had never said anything about the pain, but Benk knew. If she was quick enough, she could make it all the way down without his help, but she was too slow this time. He caught her around the waist and put her gently on the ground.

"We'll travel as traders and help wherever we can."

"No," Rose told him without hesitation. "NO," she said again with more force. "Traders don't get treated well in Yospaldo."

"We'll be careful."

There was something in his eyes that made her want to cry. She couldn't think of anything else to say. When he leaned down and kissed her on the cheek, she froze. He pulled back a couple of inches. Then he began to move his head down again, but Rose jumped away.

"I can't do it, Benk."

"Can't do what?" he asked. There was disappointment in his voice.

"I can't be normal towards men like the girls you know. I have too much in my past."

Her body was tight again. The easy mood of the Festival was gone and something in her was angry with Benk for sending it away. He was shaking his head.

"Lots of people have had hard times in their pasts. There's no reason why you can't get over your reaction to men. It was understandable in Yospaldo, but not here. You could learn to love here."

"I'll never love a man, not in that way."

Rose was so exasperated that her words were sharp, like long embroidery needles that she was sticking into Benk. Why had he done this? He ought to have known better.

"I think you should go," she added coldly.

Benk stared at her with disappointment in his eyes this time. He swung himself onto Dandy's back. "Goodbye then. I'll be back before winter." Whistling to Firefly, he was gone.

Rose stalked through the yard, yanked open the door to the Girls' Hut, slammed it shut behind her, and charged up the stairs to her room. Neither Patrise nor Melona was back. She got ready for bed and lay down, grateful for the unusual chance to hide her life from other people.

Benk will see this is for the best when he gets back. I don't want to lose his friendship, but I can't give him more.

The next day, the women in the Girls' Hut began packing what they would need for the winter. Rose was not in a good mood and she did not like the change in their routine. Every time she walked through the downstairs hall, she had to walk around a new box.

"It's not winter yet. It's fall!"

"Winter's coming," several women assured her.

"The leaves are still on the trees."

"Not for long," Melona called from the corner where she was arranging her school supplies so that what she'd need first would be on top.

Rose grumbled under her breath as she took down pictures and wrapped them in blankets.

"We can't wait until a blizzard hits," Patrise finally said in the firm tone of voice that always made Rose think she should have been a school teacher instead of Melona. "Loading the wagons in driving snow doesn't make sense."

Rose glared. Of course she didn't want to wait until a blizzard. What did Patrise think she was—stupid? Several biting comments came to mind, but if she said any of them, her temper would boil over.

"Yeah," she muttered.

Granted, it wasn't much, but she had avoided an angry rage. Maybe she was getting better. Rose finished wrapping the pictures in a better mood and offered to take over the cooking. Nobody else wanted to do it. They were all obsessed with moving inside a mountain.

Over the next two weeks, the artists barely touched their crafts. Most of their waking hours were spent packing and cleaning. More and more of the kitchen's pots and pans disappeared into boxes, but Rose managed to produce meals, though they had to stand in the kitchen and eat scrambled eggs with their fingers the last morning. The rest of the kitchen supplies had been taken to the mountain, all except for a frying pan, a spatula, and a stack of small plates that Rose had hidden under her bed.

It was nippy that morning. Rose shivered as she washed, dried and put the breakfast things into a box. While she worked, the others took the beds apart and carried the pieces to the waiting wagons. The Girls' Hut was empty now. It didn't feel like home anymore, and Rose's shoulders drooped while everyone else went into a final frenzy.

The windows had to be boarded up and the house generally prepared for high winds and icy rains. Patrise was sawing boards with her typical gusto. Melona had her mouth full of nails, which she was expertly hammering into each board as it was put in place. Leftie was caulking cracks and supervising the placement of heavy rolled-up rugs at the bottom of doors. The other women dusted, swept, and wiped. This was all a familiar part of their lives, but it was new and unsettling to Rose. At the last minute, she decided to go ahead with the wagons and make up the beds in their new place.

Get it over with.

Her face drooped as well as her shoulders during the bumpy ride. She missed Benk. He was exasperating at times, but he was also cheerful. He was critical, but he was often right in his criticisms. He was cocky, but he was also—well, cocky.

That made her smile, though her moment of cheer faded as she followed the moving crew out of fresh air and sunshine into a lantern-lit tunnel. She had to fight tears then, but those first few minutes were the hardest. The place wasn't as bad as she'd imagined it would be. There were no earthworms for one thing—at least none that she could see—and the top of the tunnel was high. She had imagined herself stooping all winter and winding up with a permanently bent back next spring.

The movers led her to the rooms set apart for the Girls' Hut and started setting up the beds. Rose waited in a corner while they worked, but when they left, she had work of her own to do. Carefully, the way Nurse Broomely had taught her, she put clean sheets on all the beds with blankets on top. Then she arranged the comforters, plumping them up to look inviting and making sure to give each woman her favorite one. By the time she finished, the cluster of caves assigned to the Girls' Hut felt more homelike, and she wandered into one of the long tunnels to explore.

The air was breathable and each tunnel was brightly lit. Rose sighed in deep relief. She didn't feel buried alive after all. It was going to be fine. She made several such sighs over the next few days—so many that Patrise started sighing deeply whenever she saw her. Rose didn't object. If she was going to be teased, she'd rather it be over her breathing habits than her worry over Benk.

He hadn't come back. He'd promised to return before

winter, but Far Reaches had moved inside the mountain, and there was no word from his group. Probably a scout thought winter started much later than she did. It was very likely, in fact. Rose told herself that several times a day. It helped at first, but as the days wore on, it helped less and less.

She found it hard to settle down with her zinnia embroidery. Melona and Patrise were eager for her to finish because they wanted to hang it on their bedroom wall, but Rose had lost interest. It took six days to do what should have taken two. When the zinnias were framed and hung, she started embroidering a picture of white daisies with yellow centers, but she couldn't keep her mind on them.

One morning she sat in her chair but couldn't make herself pick up the piece of cloth.

"I think I'll climb to the top of the mountain. The exercise will be good for me."

"It'll be cold up there. Better take a coat," Melona warned.

Rose went out into the hall and jiggled in place impatiently. Her coat was in their bedroom, which was in the opposite direction from the long winding stairs that led to the top. She forced herself to rush through the hall toward the Girls' Hut rooms. Grabbing her coat, she ran as far as she could back up the passageway. Her breathing was coming in gasps when she slowed to a walk.

"What's the hurry?" she asked herself but didn't know the answer.

It was a long climb to the top chamber. Rose struggled up until a blast of frigid wind let her know she was almost there. Shivering she threw her coat on and puffed up the final steps.

The top chamber had natural openings in the rock on all four sides. Rose braced herself against the wind and walked over to one of them. It was a spectacular view. The Far Reaches' mountain peaked far above the tree line and gave a long-ranging view of the surrounding mountains. She squinted into the wind. What were those flickering lights in the distance?

"Excuse me. Message coming through."

A squat little man pushed past her and stared intently at the lights. Rose wandered to the other openings of the chamber, but her attention kept straying back to the little man. He had stopped staring out the window and was writing something down.

"What was the message?" she asked when he stopped writing.

"Sorry, official scout news," the man said briskly.

That was a mistake.

"You have news from the scouts?" Rose marched over to him as if she would shake the news from him if he didn't tell her what it was.

The man deliberately folded the paper and put it in his pocket.

"Official!" he repeated and Rose glared at him.

"Who gets to know?"

The little man was not intimidated.

"The scouts—and their families in this case."

Chapter 12

WINTER TROUBLE

Fall came early this far north. The leaves had fallen from these trees weeks ago. It was colder here too, even in the valley. Winters must be rough. Benk sauntered into the royal barn and started sizing up the horses as any other horse trader would. He ran his hands down the front leg of a mare.

"What are you doing here?" boomed in his ear, and the master of the stable appeared at his side, frowning fiercely.

Benk straightened up with an ingratiating smile.

"Admiring your horses, Master Ricaldo. I'm a horse trader, I am, and I can't pass up seeing the best horses in Yospaldo."

Horse traders were known as smooth talkers. Benk's words poured forth convincingly, but he noticed at the same time that the mare wasn't spooked at the man's loudness. None of the horses were. They knew him better than most Yospaldons, it would seem.

"They're the best horses anywhere else too, but that doesn't mean I let strangers paw at them," growled Ricaldo.

"Yes sir, and I do understand the need for caution, sir."

While he was speaking, Benk patted the mare's neck and inconspicuously drew the outline of a fish under her mane.

"See it doesn't happen again," thundered the master, nodding very slightly. Benk wouldn't have seen the movement if he hadn't been looking for it.

"Fine herd of colts you have. Been watching them in the field and might want to talk about two of them."

"You can talk after dark then. I'm busy now," announced Ricaldo, moving off.

"After dark it is," Benk said to the broad back walking away from him.

"I'm glad to hear she made it," Ricaldo whispered that night in the privacy of his office.

The big man had to whisper. It was hard for him to lower the volume of his voice otherwise.

"She's fine. Ornery, but fine," Benk told him quietly.

"Kind of ugly though," Ricaldo mentioned, eyeing him.

Benk grinned. There was no getting anything over on this man. "She cleaned up well, but she's got issues."

"Give her time," Ricaldo said too loudly and winced. Moving back to a whisper, he told Benk, "Spies everywhere. Especially after she got away. They know someone helped her."

"Do they suspect you?"

"Don't know. I'm still alive, which indicates no."

Benk started to respond. "This place is—"

A knock on the door made both men jump.

"It's not locked," grumbled Ricaldo. "Though bothering me now, when I'm in the midst of negotiating with an idiot, is something you might want to reconsider."

The door swung open to show one of the trainers.

"I was wondering if you'd be needing anything," the man mumbled, glancing at Benk.

"No! Now leave me alone with this robber."

Benk spread his arms wide.

"I've offered fair prices. A man's got to make a living."

When the door closed, Ricaldo gripped the edge of his desk so hard his knuckles turned white.

"Spy," he whispered. "Leave this place while you can. I mean it. Go."

Benk left the stable but he had no intention of leaving Yospaldo, not when Ricaldo was in danger. He walked down the service road that wound around the back of the castle grounds to the gate. *What do you want me to do?* Getting Ricaldo away was all that came to mind. *All right. Any directions on how?*

He was halfway through the village before he said, "Got it."

When Benk entered the livery stable that had rented him a stall, Dandy raised a sleepy head. Lifting the latch on her stall door, the scout slipped in next to the mare and stroked her neck. He clenched his jaw unhappily, but it wasn't safe to linger and he couldn't take her with him now. A dog barked in a nearby yard—time to go. Grabbing his pack, he left the stable by a back door.

Early the next day, a scruffy laborer entered the door of a village diner behind what appeared to be a farmhand, judging by his smell. The diner was always crowded in the morning. People had to share tables whether they wanted to or not.

Making a face, the scruffy laborer sat beside the smelly farmhand who reeked of fertilizer, the fresh, pungent kind that came from cows. In a minute or two a merchant sat at their end of the table, peering disdainfully at both of them.

The three men placed their orders and a hurried waitress brought them cups of coffee.

"Why the new look?" asked Smelly, coughing to hide his mouth.

"Cover blown," Scruffy admitted, cup at his lips.

Scowling at the smell of manure, the merchant put a scented handkerchief to his nose.

"A man's been arrested," he said under the handkerchief.

"Who?" asked Scruffy, slurping coffee noisily.

"A palace servant, some guy they call a half-wit."

"I heard he started crying. Wanted his dad though he's

been dead for years," Smelly muttered.

Scruffy mumbled into his cup, "We've got to get Ricaldo out of this place. I've got a plan."

"Figured as much," the other two said at the same time and covered up laughter.

In between bites of eggs, toast, and bacon, Scruffy explained his plan. Questions were asked and details clarified in as few words as possible. Then the men separated.

<hr />

Ricaldo also heard about the arrest that morning from the same trainer who had poked his head into the office. The man was casual in a gossipy manner, but he was watching the head of the stable closely.

"And where's my coffee? Why are you talking to me before I get my coffee?" Ricaldo roared.

Stomping into his office, he slammed the door shut. Immediately he fell on his knees and whispered, "He's a kid on the inside, a big kid who needs help. You can do anything, Maker. Rescue him. Please. Rescue Woofy."

As he was speaking, a wagonload of hay rumbled through the castle gates into the back road that led to the stable. Wagonloads of hay were a daily occurrence on that road. They didn't warrant a second glance from the guards at the gate.

Smelly drove the wagon to the back of the stable and swung down.

"Not here—there's a lift in the stable," a boy called.

"A what?"

The boy, who was supposed to be cleaning stalls but didn't mind putting it off, led him inside the stable to a platform.

"You load the hay on this and turn the wheel. The platform lifts to the loft, where you unload it."

"Umph," Smelly grunted his thanks and the boy left.

"WHOA THERE. What in Montaland do you think you're

doing, bringing this wild grass into my stable? I want hay, not weeds."

Smelly hurried to the master's side with an ingratiating smile.

"Oh, it ain't that bad. Wild grass is better, you see. It's full of nourishment farmers don't get with pastures that are planted on year after year. The soil gets worn."

"And the soil in the wild doesn't get worn with grass growing on it year after year?" boomed Ricaldo sarcastically.

"Well, it's this way," the farmhand insisted, leaning closer and speaking confidentially—and lower so that no one could hear them. "Benk sent me to get you. There's a box in the floor of the wagon beneath the hay."

The master listened to the unfolding of the plan, his face keeping its habitual scowl.

He muttered something under his breath and then thundered, "I'm not interested in your excuses. You can take this trash away from my stable with a load of sour mash on top of it. Numskull delivered it here, of all places. Been wondering how to get rid of it and you'll do nicely. This way."

Smelly climbed into the wagon and followed Ricaldo into a dark corner that held a half dozen barrels. Several minutes passed. Then the wagon rumbled out of the barn, reeking of sour mash. Four stable hands working behind the stable held their noses as it slowly passed. The back road was empty except for one laborer, who found himself trapped between a building and the wall around the castle grounds. As the wagon drew nearer, the laborer gagged and scrambled up the back of the building, finding toeholds in the roughly hewn boards.

The fragrant wagon was waved through the main gate and told not to come back. Smelly drove down a rocky road that skirted the village and then cut through a stand of woods to more open farmland. The wagon rumbled past a couple of pastures before turning into a driveway that had weeds growing in it and potholes where the rain had made itself at home. There was an old barn at the end of the driveway. The roof of the barn had collapsed, but Smelly didn't seem to mind. He drove behind the barn and pulled to a stop.

Benk hurried out of the barn in his scruffy farmhand clothes. "You made it! Phew, that wagon reeks. Well, Ricaldo, it must have been an uncomfortable ride but—"

"He didn't come," the other scout said.

"WHAT!?"

"He refused to come, but he warned me that we'd better get out of Yospaldo fast. The sour mash was to make sure nobody stopped me."

"As if we'd leave him here," Benk scoffed, but his companion looked grim.

"Winter settles early this far north. We won't be able to travel through these mountains if we don't go soon."

"They'll either kill him or stick him in the dungeon where he'll rot," Benk told him.

The other scout's face was sad but firm. "We can't make that choice for him. If we don't leave, we'll face the same fate."

Their argument was interrupted by horses trotting on the main road, several horses from the sound of it. The farmers around here were too poor to have saddle horses. Their horses did not trot; they plodded.

Both scouts darted around the barn to a vantage point where they could see without being seen. Four burly guards had emerged from the woods and were almost past the first pasture. The scouts didn't wait to see if the men came down the old driveway. They grabbed their packs and ran through the woods behind the barn. When they reached a stream, they dashed up it, heading for their rendezvous point with the third scout, the one who had posed as a merchant.

Something didn't make sense. Benk frowned. If the guards were following the wagon, why had they let their horses trot? The guards of Yospaldo weren't the smartest people alive, but they did know how to catch people they were chasing. They wouldn't have given themselves away by the unavoidable thudding of hooves on a rocky road.

He stopped and listened. Nothing, wait—there was a muffled exclamation and a splash, as if someone had lost his footing. It could hardly be heard over the normal noise of the stream. If he hadn't stopped, Benk would never have noticed. They were being followed.

"Want to get all of us," he muttered.

The scout in front of him turned to see what was keeping Benk. He was already several yards further up the stream. Benk pointed to his ear and then down the slope. The other scout listened grimly. Then he motioned for Benk to hurry, but Benk shook his head.

"Go on," he mouthed.

The scout looked at him as if he were crazy, but Benk was used to that kind of look. He got it all the time. Pointing up the stream, he made shooing motions with his hands. The other scout hesitated, and Benk lifted his face to the sky in the posture traditionally used in Montaland to talk to the Maker. Then he made shooing motions again.

The scout nodded unhappily and left, jumping up the stream in leaps and bounds.

It was done. Benk didn't know how he'd messed up the plan, but he must have done something wrong; the Maker didn't make mistakes. He was responsible. He should bear the consequences. Swallowing hard, he reconsidered for a brief minute, unconsciously lifting his head again. Resolve flooded in, along with the strength to do what needed doing.

He didn't have his bow and arrows with him because he'd been in the role of a farmhand. Yospaldon farmhands didn't carry bows and arrows. However, they did carry slings, and there were plenty of rocks in the stream. He could delay the pursuers long enough for his friends to get away.

The guards didn't seem to like having rocks slung at them. By the time they reached Benk, the four men were sopping wet from being knocked off balance into the stream.

They took turns hitting him; then they dragged him back to the wagon and hit him some more. When he was knocked unconscious, they threw him in the wagon on top of the sour mash and headed back to Yospaldo, where they pulled him down the dungeon steps and tossed him into a cell. It was dark in the cell but not quiet. Someone was whimpering in a corner, but only a big shape could be seen.

"Shut up," one of the guards snarled.

The burly foursome dusted their hands off and left. The big shape in the corner waited until the door closed at the top of the steps. Then he shuffled over to Benk and put straw under his head. The straw was musty and old, but it provided a little cushioning. The man sat next to Benk and lifted his face, asking the Maker to make this new prisoner feel better.

<hr />

Two days later Ricaldo, a lantern in one hand and a bag in the other, snorted at the smell as he trudged down the steps that led to that part of the dungeon. The guard grunted agreement and quickly closed the door.

The stench got stronger and stronger, but the greeting at the bottom of the steps made up for it.

"Hi, hi, Ricado, hi," the man in the cell enthused, reaching through the bars with both hands.

"Hi, Woofy," he responded, putting down the lantern and grasping one of Woofy's hands.

"What'd you bring, Ricado?"

Woofy always left the "l" out of Ricaldo's name. The master of the Yospaldon stable would have roared at anyone else who did such a thing. He had never mentioned it to Woofy.

"Something to eat," he said now and Woofy beamed.

"Benk, he brought us something to eat," he told his cellmate.

"That's great," Benk said, trying to smile.

Ricaldo eyed the young man. He was weak and a cut on

his face looked bad. After sliding the food items one at a time through the bars to Woofy, Ricaldo took a flask of water from the bag and passed it to Benk, who drank thirstily.

A clean cloth came next. "Wash that cut. I brought medicine for it."

"There's no need," Benk said in a low voice.

"Now don't get like that. I'll take care of you as long as I can. We'll keep hoping," Ricaldo told him thickly.

Benk swallowed another gulp of water and whispered, "I've heard you're next. I want you to leave now and hide in that cave in the mountains I told you about. You don't need to take anything with you. It's stocked. Woofy and I'll join you tomorrow. I've got a plan."

Woofy, who was busily stuffing food into his mouth, nodded eager approval of this wise course of action.

Ricaldo cleared his throat.

"Your last plan didn't work," he pointed out with embarrassment. What else could he say? He wanted them to hope but not to have false hope.

Benk disagreed. "It worked. It just didn't work the way I thought it was going to. The Maker wanted Woofy to get out too."

Woofy beamed. "The Maker's good," he told the world.

Ricaldo looked doubtful.

"Go now," Benk said and sat down weakly. "Woofy, have you eaten all the food?"

"No, no, I saved half for you, Benk. You're my friend."

The door opened at the top of the steps, and the guard motioned to Ricaldo. Benk started to say something, but it was Woofy who had the last word.

"Obey the Maker," he told Ricaldo.

Ricaldo hesitated. Then he nodded.

<hr />

"I'll be back," Rose informed the stubborn little man.

Leaving the high chamber, she tore down the stairs. It

didn't take nearly as long going down as it had climbing up. Nor was it as demanding, but by the time she raced through the living quarters to Janna and Petten's caves, she was panting.

Janna was reading a book to the children when Rose rushed into the room.

"Where's Petten?"

"I don't know. What's the matter?" Janna asked, jumping to her feet.

"There's a message from the scouts. The ridiculous little man in the high chamber wouldn't tell me what it was."

"That's standard custom. The news has to go to the scouts first."

"He said this one would go to families too."

"That means the families of the scouts involved." Janna spoke evenly in an obvious effort to calm Rose down, but her face was taut, especially around her eyes.

Rose didn't calm down.

"How many groups haven't come back?"

"Only one," Janna admitted. There was no need to say which one. "All right, we'll help you find Petten. How about it, kids?"

"I'll check the stables," Largen said and dashed off, Tuff at his heels.

"I'll go to the meeting room," Alissa announced and then paused. "Was there a meeting today, Mom?"

"I think there was. Iris, you go with your sister and, Rose, you sit in this chair."

Rose didn't want to sit, but her legs had a different idea. They wobbled and then collapsed, making her sit with seeming obedience, though it was entirely by accident that she landed in the chair. Her hands grabbed the chair's arms.

"There's no need to get anxious," Janna said, but her own hands were nervously rubbing up and down her skirt, and Rose noted that she didn't sit anywhere. In fact, she looked as if she could barely keep herself from pacing.

The girls got back first.

"There's a meeting but Daddy's not in it," they reported breathlessly.

Janna began to gather coats.

"Then he must be at the stable area. If he's not there, we'll climb to the top chamber and I'll see what Methusenakin will tell me."

"Who?" asked Rose. She didn't smile, but the thought of a smile crossed her mind.

"Methusenakin. Don't ask me where he got that name, but he's quite proud of it, I assure you!" Janna said, trying to grin.

Without warning, Rose burst into tears. Janna and the girls patted her on the back and told her they were certain everything would be fine, but she didn't believe them and cried on.

Janna pushed something warm into her hands. "Drink this cup of tea. It'll make you feel better."

"I can't drink tea when Benk is dead," Rose wailed frantically.

"What's this?" someone asked from the door.

"Petten, thank the Maker you're here," Janna almost shouted in her relief. "What was the message Methusenakin got this morning? Have you heard it?"

"Yes," Petten said with an uneasy expression as he and his two boys came into the room. Janna stared at him before reaching for the arms of the chair next to Rose and lowering herself into it.

"Tell us," she said.

"We sent six men to the general region around Yospaldo. Three of them located and stocked a hidden cave. They're on their way home now. The other three went directly into Yospaldo in separate roles."

Petten paused and gazed intently at his wife, as if willing her strength.

"Two of those three sent the message. They've left Yospaldo without Benk."

"What happened?" Rose asked, not recognizing her own voice.

Petten turned his intent gaze upon her, but now it was as if he were deliberating how much to say.

"I think you should tell her everything. Rose loves Benk," Janna said softly.

Tears started rolling down Rose's cheeks again. She shuddered violently but didn't deny Janna's words.

"They were being followed. Benk dropped back to give the other two time to get away."

"Who was following them?" whispered Rose.

"Palace guards."

The room was still there. It should have gone dim and faded away, but it was still there. Rose could see everything in it distinctly. The rocking chair by the fire was off place. They needed to put it back where it belonged. She stared fixedly at a picture on the wall before realizing it was one of her own embroideries. She remembered doing that one. It was wild roses climbing a gate. They were pink, those roses. She had seen them on a gate in Mount Pasture when she and Benk were leaving the kingdom. Benk had been mad at her that day.

Slowly she became aware of people talking around her.

"Lift her feet onto this."

"Her hands are cold."

People were rubbing lotion on her hands. Why were they doing that? Her hands weren't hurt. It was her feet that had gotten hurt. Wasn't that right?

"Rose!" someone called and she jerked her head. "The Maker will take care of him."

She didn't quit trembling. How long had she been trembling?

The someone caught hold of her hands and Rose remembered her name this time. Janna—that was it. She was talking. Maybe Rose should listen.

"Benk told me once that he always asks the Maker for help in tough situations. That's how he comes up with so many crazy plans."

Petten added, "And that's why his plans work, even though they seem crazy."

Rose opened her mouth and a question came out. "What are the scouts going to do?"

When Petten didn't answer, she tried again. "How are they going to rescue Benk?"

"The two that escaped the guards can't go back. They've been exposed. They can't get to Far Reaches either. They made it part way, but an early blizzard has made the mountains impassable. They'll have to stay where they are."

"But what about Benk?" asked little Iris, starting to sob.

"The Maker will help him," her big sister said. Alissa was standing with her hands on her hips. She didn't like to see everyone so upset; even her brothers were crying. Well, of course they were. They adored Benk.

"The Maker will help," she said again, louder this time as if the louder she said it, the truer it was.

When she grew up, Alissa became a healer, but a very different kind of healer from Windola. Alissa loved being with people and she was very effective in helping them, but she never tolerated crying very well.

"He will," Petten agreed.

"Yes," said Rose and stood shakily. She wanted to go back to her room and be by herself.

"We'll let you know if there's more news," Janna said through her own tears.

"Yes."

Moving to her side, Petten put a hand on one of her elbows. "I'll see you to your room."

Rose didn't talk over the next month and a half. She'd say an occasional monosyllable, but that was all. She picked at her food. Everyone was worried about her and all those worried individuals hovered around, giving advice or trying to comfort. As a consequence, Rose remained in a constant state of annoyed irritability.

Melona and Patrise encouraged her to keep on embroidering; Leftie ordered her to. The end result was that Rose began avoiding the craft room altogether. Every morning she climbed the long stairs that led to the high chamber. When she reached the top, she went straight to the natural window that had carried the last message from the scouts, not that they had been the ones to flash those particular lights. Rose knew now there were relay systems set up in every direction. The scouts had sent their message to one station that had sent it on to another and another until it reached them.

She stood in the opening as long as she could take the icy winds and freezing temperatures, staring over the white expanse. Her winter coat took up permanent residence in the small room close to the top. No one objected, though the room with its warm fire was meant for the exclusive use of the four Far Reachers who knew how to send and receive messages. The message crew normally took shifts of four hours each. The shifts shortened to one hour when the temperature dipped below freezing. They stopped altogether during a blizzard. Winds gusted so powerfully then that anyone foolish enough to step into the upper chamber would be swept out a window as if he—or she—was a feather.

Whenever a blizzard struck, the message experts huddled near the fire and kept a lookout for Rose. They wanted to stop her from climbing up to the top and becoming a feather. She always glowered at them, which prompted them to explain again how dangerous it was. Rose understood the situation well enough, but she couldn't seem to keep herself from glowering, and she developed a strong dislike for blizzards, winds, and even feathers.

There were no messages in blizzards. Unfortunately

there weren't any in good weather either, but Rose felt better when someone was in the high chamber watching for them, and she preferred that someone to be Methusenakin. He had a business-like manner. Whenever she entered the high chamber, he would say, "Hello there. You again! No news yet."

Rose would nod and go to her opening. Methusenakin never asked her to move. After a while, one of the message crew would bring her a cup of hot tea. Rose would sip the drink, staring into the snow until her eyes hurt. When her body started feeling numb, she would shuffle over to the stairs. Then she'd glance back. Methusenakin would say briskly, "The moment we hear—yes!"

It wasn't Janna who helped Rose recover from the shock of the bad news. Janna had known Benk since he was born. He had teased her, fought with her, and helped rescue her from the fernpeople years ago. When he came to Far Reaches as a scout-in-training, she'd treated him like a kid brother, having him up for so many meals that Petten and the children adopted him as a member of the family. She and Rose shared the bond of deep caring, but there were times when they didn't want to be with each other. The worry that already went deep, would go a little deeper then.

Windola was the one who finally got through to Rose. The quiet self-effacing healer hadn't visited very often over the summer. At first when she came into town for supplies, she'd dropped by the craft shop to check on Rose's feet, but as time passed, she'd quit coming. After the move into the mountain, she tended to the sick and otherwise kept to herself.

When she walked into Rose's bedroom one morning in the middle of winter, Rose was startled into speech.

"What are you doing here?"

It was a throwback to one of the abrupt comments Rose used to make. She'd learned how to talk to people in a more friendly fashion, but the healer ignored her question and went straight to the point.

"You're making yourself sick."

"I don't care," Rose muttered. Her eyes wandered away.

"It has to stop."

Windola had never spoken to her this emphatically. Rose's eyes swung back to her in surprise.

"Why?" she asked flatly.

"You'll want to be well if Benk gets back. If he doesn't, he'll be in the high home—happy."

Rose considered this.

If Benk gets back safely, then yes, I'd want to be well. If he has died—that's what Windola is really saying— then he's happy. He's perfectly happy in the high home.

"That's awful!" she said loudly and immediately tried to pull herself together.

Windola had always been able to do this to her and she had never liked it. Surely all gut-level reactions weren't meant to be exposed, but there wasn't any point in trying to hide anything from this woman.

"You don't understand. I was angry with Benk the last time we saw each other. He wanted to kiss me and I wouldn't let him. I told him it could never be that way between us. I was sharp with him, and he left not knowing that ..."

Rose blinked hard to keep back the tears.

"He knows."

"What does he know?" Rose asked, leaning forward. How did Windola find out these things?

"He knows that you love him," Windola said, making a real effort to be wordy. "Benk's smart. He wasn't going to rush you; that's all."

"But I told him it was impossible."

Windola shook her head.

"Another thing about Benk. He's stubborn."

Rose stared at her. The first smile she had given anyone in weeks played around her lips. Windola was certainly right about that. Benk was as stubborn as they came. He wouldn't have given up when Rose put him off. He would have simply tried again another time.

They sat there smiling at each other while Rose thought it through. Then the healer got briskly up.

"It's lunchtime."

Rose considered saying she wasn't hungry, but what was the use?

"Benk's not the only stubborn one around here," she commented as she got up.

———— ⌒⌒⌒ ————

After that Rose ate more normally and slept better. The long months of winter passed one by one. She started checking with Petten every morning, because he could tell her if a blizzard was raging. There was no point in climbing the stairs those days. She went into the craft room instead and embroidered.

The zinnia picture was hanging on a wall in their bedroom. Two small daisy pictures brightened up the wall opposite the zinnias, because Melona and Patrise had insisted on keeping those embroideries too.

"Rose needs them," Patrise told Leftie in a sweet, selfless tone of voice as they worked in the craft room one day.

"Ha!" was Leftie's response. "You don't mind having them there yourself."

"That's true," agreed Patrise, losing the sweet selflessness.

Rose laughed along with the others, but she knew her friend had decided not to hang her latest impressionistic painting of a fir tree in a snow blizzard because she didn't think Rose needed to be reminded of blizzards. Patrise might be totally and completely wrong concerning art—but she was kind.

Everyone settled down to work. Thirty minutes passed. Rose had busily cut a new piece of material and stretched it onto an embroidery hoop. That had taken ten minutes. The rest of the time she had sat in her chair with the material in her lap, staring at it.

Patrise?" she finally asked.

"Yes?"

When Rose didn't respond right away, the impressionist put down her paintbrush and stretched.

"I want to do a tree, but I don't know them. There was a tree behind the musicians at the Fall Festival, a tall golden one. Did you see it?"

"I saw a hundred others like it."

"The sun shone on this one. It glowed!"

Patrise was enthusiastic. "That would make a beautiful embroidery."

"But I don't know trees. I know how to do flowers, but I've never done a tree. I haven't studied them," Rose wailed.

"Listen to me," Patrise said in her school teacher voice. "I know we have different ideas on art, but you just listen to me this once. It's not necessary to get the tree exactly right in every detail. You're a good enough artist to make it look like a tree. We both know that. Concentrate on how it glowed and then embroider the glow on to your page. It doesn't matter if the tree isn't exactly right."

"Yes it does! It'll be horrible if it isn't exactly right, but—I don't seem to have a choice. I can't get my mind on anything else."

"Try it," encouraged Patrise.

"I'll consider it," Rose said grumpily and slouched in her chair, frowning at the floor.

Patrise went back to work. After a few minutes, Rose bent over her box of colored thread. Holding up a shade of gold and a shade of yellow to the light, she examined them. Then she caught sight of Patrise watching and threw them back into the box. The painter turned her head away quickly, but there was a smirk on her face.

Rose slouched in her chair again, but Patrise was no longer looking so what was the point? Before long, all the yellow and gold threads were on the table, as well as several grays, browns, and blacks, with seven different shades of blue for the sky. Rose no longer cared what Patrise was doing. She was too busy trying to remember what her tree had looked like.

The dark outlines of a trunk and branches took shape, and over the next few days ground and sky emerged with no problem. When she started on the yellow and gold leaves, however, she began to feel uncomfortable and decided to talk it over with Janna.

"I've always felt a partnership with the Maker when I work. Any artist does if they're being honest, but now, putting the glow into these leaves I feel such a big dose of it."

Janna smiled and Rose knew what she was going to say.

"And don't say how wonderful that is. It's not right. It's simply not right!"

"That's ridiculous," Janna said calmly.

"No, it isn't. You don't know how mixed up I am inside—and don't say we all are or I'll know you don't really understand."

Janna made a face. "Will you quit telling me what I can or can't say? It's inhibiting!"

Rose had to laugh at her friend's wry expression, but she didn't change her mind.

"Benk knew. He told me after that disastrous visit to Mount Pasture that I was pretty on the outside but ugly on the inside."

Janna unexpectedly agreed. "Of course you were. You might have known about what the Maker did for us, but you didn't know him, not him himself, if you see what I mean, and it's getting to know him that changes us. Even then it's a matter of jumping forward and stumbling backward, but he's overseeing the whole thing. Somehow we grow."

Rose wasn't convinced.

"I see qualities I admire in other people. Melona is sweet and patient. Patrise is kind and sensitive. Windola is wise. You are all those things."

Janna hooted with laughter but Rose wasn't finished.

"The times I feel kind or patient or wise don't last. I go back to being angry or rude or jealous in a twinkling."

"It doesn't show," Janna said.

Rose stared sternly at her, and Janna revised her comment.

"Most of the time. In any case, that's what happens to everyone who's trying to be better. We know the yuck inside but other people don't. If we try to hide the yuck and pretend it's not there, it's unhealthy. What we've got to do is be honest and keep jumping. Two jumps forward, one stumble backward."

Rose frowned. "You make it sound like a hopscotch game."

"That it is," Janna agreed, standing up. Hopscotch reminded her of her children who were visiting Petten at the stables. He should need rescuing by now. "You'll be fine as long as you don't forget who's in charge of the game!"

"Yeah yeah, but—"

"Now see here, Rose," Janna interrupted, placing her hands on her hips.

She looked like her oldest daughter when she did that, and a lighthearted feeling sprang up inside of Rose. It had been a long time since she'd felt lighthearted.

"If the Maker is blessing your tree embroidery with a special feeling of partnership, why can't you enjoy it—and wipe that grin off your face!"

"You look just like Alissa when you do that," Rose said, continuing to grin.

"I do NOT look like Alissa. SHE looks like ME," and with that Janna swept out of the room.

Rose carried the lighthearted feeling back to the embroidery room. She was now putting very pale shades of gold and yellow amongst the brighter ones. The leaves around the tree started to glow. Then the air around the leaves glowed too. Late afternoon sunshine was supposed to be streaming in to brighten up the tree, but the glow was more than that.

She didn't realize how much extra time she was spending in the craft room until Leftie mentioned it one morning approvingly. Rose promptly stuck her needle in the fabric and folded it.

"What are you doing?" Leftie asked in a disgruntled manner.

"I'm going to the high chamber. I skipped two days because of the weather and I got caught up in my embroidery yesterday. It's been three and a half days!"

"Lunch is in a few minutes. Why don't you embroider now and go this afternoon?"

"My tree's done," Rose answered slowly, unfolding the fabric again and holding it up for Leftie to see. She hadn't allowed anyone to look at it before now, not even the other crafts people.

Leftie gazed at it in awe.

"That's the prettiest one you've ever done. It's more than pretty, but I don't know how to say it."

"I do," said Patrise, who had dashed from her painting to stand by Leftie. "It's glory, Rose. You've put glory into that tree."

"It wasn't me who put it there and it's not the tree's glory!" answered Rose a little crustily.

"Well," began Patrise, but Leftie suddenly shrieked. "Patrise, you're dripping paint on my knitting!"

Rose made her escape in the chaos that followed. She didn't want to wait until after lunch. How could she have neglected her trek to the high chamber for this long! Climbing the stairs in a rush, she grabbed her coat from the small room near the top, moving quietly so she wouldn't disturb the off-duty message expert who was snoring in his chair. Methusenakin was in the high chamber. "Hello there. It's you again! No news yet."

Rose walked across to her favorite opening.

"What's happened?" she asked quickly.

The frozen white of winter was sharp and clear on the high mountain, but the air was hazy and indistinct everywhere else.

Methusenakin came to stand next to her. "Spring has arrived in the lower altitudes. The snow is melting and there's moisture in the air."

Without warning there was a flicker of light. Rose gasped and Methusenakin almost fell out of the opening in his eagerness to decipher the message. The flickers went on for a long time. Rose knew better than to interrupt his concentration, but she was frantic to know what the message was when the flickers finally ended.

"What—" she said, but Methusenakin was rushing to the bright lantern always kept burning in the center of the room.

"Move," he ordered as he ran back to the opening.

Quickly the little man flashed a message of his own, using the light and its shuttered closing to make the different symbols. He waited stiffly. When the answer came back, he wrote it down with painstaking exactness. Then he turned to Rose.

She didn't speak again. She couldn't. Methusenakin wasn't supposed to tell her the message, and even though Rose knew she'd hear it eventually through Janna, she didn't think she could survive the wait. Her eyes begged.

"The two scouts who reported in the spring have made it through the winter. They are on their way back to Far Reaches. That was the gist of the first message," the little man announced importantly.

Rose couldn't speak. What had happened to Benk?

"I sent them a message asking about the missing scout," Methusenakin said next, but his eyes shifted away while he said it.

Rose's heart clunked down onto the chamber floor.

"There is no new information."

He was looking at her now as if he didn't know what

she might do next. Rose didn't blame him. She didn't know what she might do next either. She needed to pick up her heart from the floor, but her body was refusing to move. Methusenakin interrupted this interesting dilemma.

"It was not to be expected that they would hear from him. They were at one place. He was at another."

"The dungeon," she croaked despairingly.

Methusenakin drew himself up to a business-like stance.

"I am assuming that the young man in question has been out of the dungeon long before now. Escape would have been in character for him, and we should expect someone who is absent to act in character. After his escape, he would have found a place to spend the winter. He could not have gotten in touch with us, because he would no longer have the necessary equipment. Eventually he will come himself."

It is doubtful whether Methusenakin had received very many hugs from attractive young women. When Rose rushed at him, he didn't know what to do with his arms. It was only after she had dashed from the chamber that he returned to a proper consciousness of his official duty. He woke up the other message expert, told him to take his place in the high chamber, and walked briskly down the steps to deliver his message. It wasn't until he'd almost reached the scouts' living quarters that he realized he was whistling.

Instantly he closed his lips and put on the solemn expression that should accompany his report. It was a good thing he had been given permission to tell Rose the message. He might have been tempted to break a rule if they hadn't—and that would have been out of character.

Chapter 13

Spring

The two scouts got home a week ahead of Far Reaches' scheduled spring move. There was an atmosphere of exuberant joy everywhere inside the mountain. Rose had to force herself to smile. She was glad these men were safely back. She certainly didn't wish them to be dead or suffering, but where was Benk? If he'd escaped the dungeon and wintered somewhere, why wasn't he home now too?

The week slowly passed and the day of the big move arrived. Wagons pulled in and pulled out, carrying people and their belongings. The further away they lived, the earlier they got to go because of the longer travel time. That way everyone got home during the day, which made unpacking easier. The Girls' Hut was one of the closer houses. Consequently the women who lived there didn't arrive home until early evening.

"It's good to be back," Melona said comfortably.

Melona, Patrise, and Rose were standing in their bedroom at the Girls' Hut, staring at a jumble of boxes. The beds had been set up, but the mattresses weren't very inviting without sheets and blankets. Patrise shivered.

"Why did we have to move this early? It's cold in here."

"I'll light a fire. That'll warm us," Melona assured her.

She busied herself with the fire, while Patrise started

sorting boxes. Rose opened the one marked 'Sheets and Bedspreads' and silently made up the beds. Patrise and Melona talked cheerfully to each other, not seeming to notice Rose's lack of enthusiasm. A bell rang downstairs.

"Hooray! It's suppertime," shouted Patrise.

Everyone but Rose chattered as they ate around the Girls' Hut table. Then they chattered as they cleaned up after the meal.

There's something about a move that makes people talk. Won't they ever stop?

The house wasn't quiet until late that night. Then it became too quiet. Rose lay in bed, listening to the silence. All things considered, she preferred the chattering. It was more distracting. She pulled the covers to her chin and closed her eyes. Why not! There was nothing to see with them open. The boards over the windows were still in place. They provided protection from the cold night breezes, but they also blocked any light.

Rose missed the moonlight. She started crying listlessly and couldn't stop.

"Rose?" Melona put her feet down on the cold floor and lit a candle. "Oh Rose, don't cry."

"What is it?" asked a grumpy voice.

"It's Rose."

Patrise pushed herself up and sat, surveying the situation. "She's been sad all day."

"I'll go downstairs and heat a pot of milk," Melona said.

Rose wanted to tell her not to bother, but she couldn't muster the energy. Patrise came over and sat on her bed.

"We shouldn't have left the mountain this early. You were settled in the caves. It's upset you to make the move."

Melona was rattling around in the kitchen. Then she exclaimed and they could hear her opening the outside door. Booming words rolled up the stairs and into their room.

"Hello, miss. I'm trying to find a girl your age. Name's Rose. Is this the place called the Girls' Hut?"

Rose had her feet on the floor with the first word and was hurtling down the stairs by the time he said her name.

"Ricaldo?" she whispered at the door to the kitchen.

The big man's face lit up at the sight of her. She flew towards him and for the second time that spring gave a hug to someone who was not accustomed to receiving them.

The other inhabitants of the Girls' Hut were awake by then. They hurried downstairs, edging past the stranger talking to Rose in the doorway. Leftie stumbled over Patrise's foot and both of them had to hold onto the kitchen table to keep from falling. Melona slipped Rose's arms into a robe, tying the warm garment closely around her.

Rose wasn't aware any of them were there. As far as she was concerned, she and Ricaldo were alone.

"How did you get away from Yospaldo? Did you hear any news of someone called Benk? He was probably in the dungeon."

Seeing Ricaldo brought back unpleasant memories of the Yospaldon palace. Rose could hear the shrieks of prisoners. Her lips trembled and she felt like putting her fingers in her ears, but fingers wouldn't stop memories. Her face turned white with the effort to quit remembering.

Ricaldo stared at her with a worried frown. "I guess she was right. You did need to know even though it's the middle of the night."

He guided her over to a chair by the table. Melona had to scurry to one side, but she scurried unnoticed. Everyone's attention was fixed on Ricaldo, who pushed Rose gently down and sat in the chair next to her with a tired thump.

"Did I know someone named Benk? I certainly did. He got me out of the worst mess I've ever been in and that's saying a lot. It would have been me in the dungeons for sure, if he hadn't told me where to go and when. You see, the Yospaldon higher-ups were furious when you escaped. Someone in the palace must have helped you, they figured, and they were on the watch for who that might be. They also checked on every stranger who came to town. That's why they became suspicious of the scouts.

"I warned Benk and he made plans to get me away, but things got complicated. Woofy had been thrown in the dungeon, poor guy, and I couldn't leave him. He was one of us, the Maker's people, and I was the only person with enough clout to bring him food and water. Turns out, they'd suspected me all along and were gonna make a public example of me. Benk discovered this somehow, even in the dungeon. That young man could squeeze news from dry wood. He told me to go to a cave where the scouts had stored supplies. He and Woofy would join me the next day after they escaped. I went, but I didn't think I'd ever see them again.

"In the morning I started back towards Yospaldo. I don't know what I was planning to do. Storm the castle? It was crazy, but I felt a pull and went with it, thinking the Maker might be directing me. The closer I got to Yospaldo, the more nervous I felt. I was ready to make tracks back to my hiding place, when Woofy popped from behind a bush and waved at me."

He stopped talking and cleared a hoarse throat.

"Can I have something to drink?"

Rose didn't move. She was barely breathing. Leftie gave Ricaldo a glass of cold water, and he drank fast in a series of gulps that were quite audible in the silent room. Then he continued.

"Benk was with Woofy, but he'd collapsed. He was in bad shape, you see. They starve their prisoners in addition to beating—"

Rose stood abruptly. Melona slipped an arm around her trembling shoulders, and Patrise put the full authority of a school teacher on her face.

"Where's Benk at this moment? That's what Rose wants to know. Where is he? She doesn't need to hear all those other things."

"Squash me for a horse fly," Ricaldo moaned. "I'm sorry,

girl. You already know more than you want to about that place. Woofy and I carried him to the hiding place and took care of him over the winter. It wasn't what I'd call an easy time, but we made it and then headed for Far Reaches. I left Benk in a healer's cabin. Windola was her name. She sent me here double-time to tell you where he is."

Rose sank into her chair and covered her face. Almost immediately, she hopped up again and started for the door.

"Hold on," Ricaldo said as his hands grabbed her shoulders and stopped her.

"You're not to visit tonight. Windola wants him to sleep. You can see him tomorrow. Understand?"

She nodded dumbly. Benk was in Far Reaches and Windola was taking care of him. A smile broke over her face, but it was a wet one. Rose, who hated emotional displays, couldn't control herself. She began to laugh and cry at the same time, going into hysterics as smoothly as if she did it every day.

The women in the Girls' Hut had stayed admirably quiet during Ricaldo's story. That quiet was now officially over.

"Get her a handkerchief. Who's got clean handkerchiefs unpacked?"

"I'll make hot chocolate. Reach down that pot."

"I knew Benk would escape. Trust that boy to get into trouble and then out of it again."

"Is there any leftover cake? We need to celebrate!"

"Follow me; I'll take you to the scout's house."

The last remark was directed toward Ricaldo, who energetically jumped from his chair to follow the speaker. He had perked up at the mention of cake, but there were too many women talking at one time in that kitchen. It was better to get away now and have cake later.

Rose let people hug her and wipe her face with the kitchen towel that was being used as a substitute for a handkerchief. Obediently drinking her cup of hot chocolate, she said it didn't matter when no cake could be found. Eventually everyone went back to bed. She lay in the darkness, no sleepier than she'd been before, but this time she knew where Benk was. He was with Windola and ...

To her surprise, Rose slept deeply the rest of the night. She woke early the next morning, hopped out of bed, and threw on the same clothes she'd worn yesterday. They were so convenient. Her hair was probably all right. She'd slip away and—

"Where do you think you're going in that state? Get back in this room and brush your hair! Gracious highlands! Your shirt's on inside out! Melona, get her another shirt. That one's too plain."

"I'm fine, Patrise. It doesn't matter what I look like."

"Don't even think of that stupid apple thing. It's too early in the morning for metaphors. You can't go to see Benk looking as if you just got up!" growled Patrise.

"I DID just get up."

Grabbing the brush from Patrise's outstretched hand, Rose swiped at her hair. With frantic haste, she took off her shirt and put it on again, with the right side out this time. Buttoning her jumper was done in a flash, but she missed a button and had to do the whole thing over. Then she flew from the room, ignoring Patrise's command to wear the pretty shirt Melona had found. Groaning in unison, Patrise and Melona fell back into their beds, but Rose was out of the Girls' Hut and flying down the village street before they could pull the covers up.

It wasn't until she reached the edge of the village that Rose realized she didn't know how to go through the woods to Windola's cabin. Fortunately for her, a rider was coming along the road behind her. She waved wildly at him. When he got closer, she saw that it was Ricaldo.

"Want a lift?" he asked, grinning at her and she smiled sheepishly back.

"I don't know how to get there," she admitted.

He pulled her up onto the horse behind him. "I'm not sure

I do either. It was dark when I came to find you last night. At least I've got a horse under me now. We'll get there."

Ricaldo must have had a good sense of direction. With no trouble at all, he rode directly to Windola's cabin and helped Rose off the horse. Her heart was beating double time as she took two quick steps toward the cabin door. Then she stopped short. Benk might be asleep. Maybe she should sit on the doorstep until she heard someone moving around in there.

I told him there was no way I could care for a man.

Coming this early was bold and pushy; that's what it was. She should have given him more time to recuperate and then shown up with a nice batch of cookies. That would have been normal. Why couldn't she ever act like a normal person!

I can't go in there.

Ricaldo knew of no reason why not! He tied the horse to a tree and strode up to the cottage door, propelling Rose in front of him.

"Anybody awake in there?" he bellowed.

"We are now," someone said cheerfully, and Rose's throat swelled.

Ricaldo opened the cottage door, pushing her into the familiar kitchen. Benk was lying on the couch she had occupied less than a year ago. He studied her for a moment.

"Did you bring me something good to eat?"

"No," she whispered, blinking fast.

If I cry right now, I will die. I will simply die. It's embarrassing enough to have—

Benk had a long-suffering, self-righteous look on his face. "What kind of a visit is this? You know Windola doesn't make anything but soup. You should have brought cookies."

Windola came into the room then.

"Tea?" she asked Rose in her quiet way.

"Yes, please," managed Rose, collapsing into a kitchen chair.

"How're the feet?" asked Benk next.

He was thin, there was a scar on his face, and one arm was in a sling. Rose swallowed. *You will not, absolutely NOT, cry now. Sit up straight. PRETEND to be normal.* "They're healed. I walked a lot this winter, and they never gave me any trouble."

"You can't tell me you walked a lot in the Far Reaches' caves. There's nowhere to go."

Rose corrected him indignantly. "I did walk a lot. Almost every day, I climbed to the high chamber. It, it had a nice view."

"I know why you went there," Benk said in a low voice.

Rose stared at the floor, blinking hard again.

There was a moment of silence. Then Benk remarked casually, "You are a little skinny, at that. Too much stair-climbing, I'd guess. You'll have to make cookies and gain weight. I'll be happy to sample them for you."

Rose exchanged a smile with Windola.

"I'll make cookies, you greedy man, but I can't do everything at once. I wanted to see how you were first."

"Oh, I'm fine. I just decided to take a break from work," Benk said, stretching lazily.

"Is anyone else hungry? What's for breakfast?" boomed Ricaldo.

Windola rose quietly from her chair.

"What do you need from the pantry?" Rose asked.

"A few eggs." Windola's eyes strayed to Ricaldo's large form dwarfing one of her chairs. "All the eggs."

They started with porridge before moving on to scrambled eggs and toast. There was wild blackberry jam for the toast and plenty of Windola's famous tea. Ricaldo and Benk ate as if they were never going to stop. When they finally pushed away from the table, Windola had dismay in her eyes.

"I'll bring extra supplies from the village," Rose offered, but Ricaldo shook his head.

"I'm going to eat at the scout house. I'll be living there from now on. Got a nice room to myself! They want me to help with horse training. You'll only have Benk to feed, Windola, though that might be quite a job considering how much he ate at this one meal."

"How much I ate—you hogged the toast," Benk said indignantly.

"I did not! Besides, you had most of the honey and cream on your porridge and your bowl was bigger than mine."

They squabbled back and forth, like two little boys. Rose listened contentedly and smiled again at Windola.

Three days later Benk moved back to the scout house. He asked Rose offhandedly if she wanted to go to the Spring Festival with him.

"Got to beat Dalc again."

"As if I'd go with him."

Rose lifted her nose and sniffed.

"He's not bad," Benk admitted. "Did you know Woofy's working for him now? Woofy likes farms. His father was a farmer."

Rose was instantly subdued. "I hadn't heard. That's good of Dalc."

"Yeah well, I'll let you off if you want to go to the festival with him," teased Benk.

He was constantly teasing these days. He never said anything to her in the low voice that meant he was speaking from the heart.

Rose didn't like it. She didn't like it at all, but she had no idea how to let him know she'd changed her mind. The Yospaldon ladies flirted and paid a lot of attention to their hair and dresses. Whatever they did had to be wrong, but what was right? She couldn't figure it out.

Alland had arrived to check on his little brother, his family in tow. His two daughters were sweet gentle girls. Rose liked them. She liked Alland too. The tall shepherd reminded her of Benk, always joking and teasing people. Alland's wife, however, was another matter. Rose had forgotten how beautiful the grown-up Alissa was. *She's Janna's best friend. Janna named her first baby girl after her.*

Rose tried to stifle her jealousy, but when she heard that the Mount Pasture family had squeezed into Janna's cabin for their visit, she wanted to grind her teeth.

I haven't stumbled back. I've made a backward somersault.

When Janna invited Rose and Benk for supper two days before the Spring Festival, Rose accepted half-heartedly. She could feel an ugly mood rising and was afraid she'd be rude. Benk must have been thinking along the same lines. As soon as they left the Girls' Hut, he started lecturing.

"I don't want to see any bad behavior tonight. There's no excuse for it. Alland is my oldest brother and Alissa is one of the loveliest women you could ever hope to meet."

"I've never hoped to meet any lovely women," she snapped, which didn't get the evening off to a promising start.

The young stallion Benk was riding snorted at something scurrying through the underbrush, and Rose thought of a change of subject.

"That must be your new horse—a gray one this time. You do go through horses, Benk. Whatever happened to Dandy?"

Benk exhaled unhappily, and Rose could have bitten her tongue off. She had tried very hard not to ask questions that would bring back painful memories of his time in Yospaldo. She'd been considerate for days.

We're five minutes into the evening, and I've already ruined it.

"I don't know," Benk mumbled eventually.

"She'll be fine. Yospaldons don't treat people well, but they love horses," Rose said quickly.

"Yeah," Benk replied and stayed silent the rest of the trip.

By the time they arrived and the two families came outside to greet them, Rose's ugly mood had subsided into a semblance of good manners. She ate the meal and laughed at the jokes that flew rapidly back and forth across the table. Even when the grown-up Alissa, beautiful as ever, spoke directly to her, she tried to respond pleasantly.

Benk nodded his approval, but it seemed to Rose there was a reserve in his eyes. She didn't blame him for not trusting her. Maybe he didn't want to be her friend any longer.

When Petten offered to take the children on a hike after supper, Janna accepted eagerly.

"I'll do the dishes. You do the children!"

"I'll do the children too," volunteered Benk, who hated washing dishes. Alland wanted to be with Benk, so off the hikers went leaving Rose alone with Janna and Alissa.

The two older women worked well together. Alissa washed the dishes, plunging her smooth hands unhesitatingly into the hot soapy water. Rose dried and Janna put everything up. Rose got quieter and quieter as they worked. Janna and Alissa had no trouble carrying the conversation though, and as they talked Rose couldn't help but see how close they were. When Janna mentioned a discipline problem she was having with her children, Alissa gave the considered answer of someone who had experienced it too.

They're the same age. People need friends who are the same age. It was a very wise observation, she felt, but it wasn't an especially encouraging one, not under the circumstances. Her jealousy was being dampened but only by sadness.

I don't deserve a best friend.

After the dishes, Janna led them into the family room where a fire was crackling. As soon as Alissa sat down, she turned to Rose.

"I have been hoping for an opportunity to tell you how much I appreciate you," she said warmly.

"Why?" Rose asked bluntly.

"It is obvious that Benk loves you," Alissa answered with a smile that Rose subjected to an instant credibility test. She wasn't laughing at her. Rose was almost certain she wasn't— but Alissa was continuing.

"Alland and I had begun to think that he would never find a woman he could love. Many girls have liked him, but he has never liked them back, not in that special way, not in the way he cares for you."

Rose started crying. She couldn't believe it. What a baby! Savagely she wiped her cheeks dry.

"He ought not to," she told the two women in front of her, who were looking at her with deep concern in their eyes.

A loud hullabaloo from the yard announced the hikers' arrival home.

"I'll take care of this," Janna said and left the room.

Rose and Alissa could hear her clearly.

"Stop right where you are," she shouted in no uncertain terms. "We need privacy in here. Alland, make yourself useful. Play tag with everyone."

The children greeted the prospect of tag with a whoop of joy. To Rose's surprise, the two loudest whoops came from Alissa's sweet little girls. Janna's children obviously brought out a whole new side to them. Janna whooped along with the children and called a few further directions to the adults. "Watch Alland, Benk. He cheats at tag. Leaping lambs, I can't believe I told YOU that, of all people! Petten, keep an eye on both Alland and Benk. They come from a long line of tag cheaters!"

The brothers yelled denials, but Janna ignored them and came grinning back into the room. Rose had quit crying by then and was sitting bolt upright with a determined expression on her face. As soon as Janna sat down, she began.

"I don't deserve Benk's love or your friendship. I've been jealous from the moment I met you, Alissa, because you're Janna's best friend. I was sure you'd be a horrible person because of your beauty. You're not horrible; you're kind and warmhearted, but I was so jealous that I hated you. Janna, I liked you from the start, but I wanted you to be my friend and nobody else's. To tell the truth, I think I've been jealous of you too. Everyone loves you. Everyone in the village feels close to you. I would've pushed them all away if I could have. There's no excuse for my bad feelings. I am a spiteful, self-centered person."

Rose shut her mouth and wished she could shut her eyes too. She had made herself confess these things, but now she wanted to leave. Neither Janna nor Alissa would ever want to be with her again.

"I know exactly what you mean," both of those women said at the same time and then laughed at each other.

"I've wished I could look and be like Alissa ever since I first met her. You should have seen me in the Fern Queen's palace. I know what jealousy is," Janna confessed.

"I have always wished that I could make friends as easily as Janna does. You are right, Rose. Everyone is her close friend. I don't know how she does it, but I too have been jealous," was Alissa's contribution.

Rose's lips wanted to fall open, but she didn't let them. Instead, she stared hard at Janna and Alissa—they seemed to be telling the truth.

"But you're so old!" she found herself saying.

Alissa cleared her throat gently and Janna rolled her eyes.

"I did it again," Rose groaned, pounding the arms of her chair. "I say things wrong. What I meant was that you're both older and wiser than I am. You're wonderful people. How can you possibly have been jealous?"

Janna snorted and responded with one word—"Easily."

"It's the older people who have experienced all the bad thoughts and emotions. Hopefully we learn how to deal with them as we get older, but it's a given fact that we have known them," Alissa said.

Janna was nodding agreement. "Sure is! I haven't always had friends. When I first met Alissa, everyone in Mount Pasture was angry at me. I felt very alone."

Rose was feeling happier. In fact, as long as she was baring her soul, why not do a thorough job!

"One more question," she said quickly, knowing their

time together was limited. The tag players had to be stopped before anyone else died. Two or three had passed away already, judging by the intense screams coming from the yard.

"How does someone let someone else know she's interested in him?" Rose made herself ask.

The women moved their chairs closer to hers. The three of them bent their heads together.

<hr>

Two days later Janna and Alissa walked into the Girls' Hut and up the stairs toward Rose's bedroom. As they reached the second floor, Melona and Patrise stumbled from the room and stared glassy-eyed in their direction.

"Good luck," Patrise whispered as if they would need it.

Melona didn't say anything, but she held onto to the railing with both hands as she started down the stairs.

"What happened?" Janna asked but neither sister seemed able to answer.

Janna and Alissa glanced at each other and quickly entered the room, where they found Rose standing in front of her bed, hands clenched into fists. The dress they had chosen for her was on her body. That much could be said. Every button was buttoned and the sash at the back of her dress was tied. The rich gray of the dress was wonderful against Rose's skin and black hair. The fit was perfect.

So far, so good, Janna told herself. She prepared for battle.

Rose was holding a brush in one hand, but her stance was more that of a woman wielding a weapon than a woman brushing her hair. Her brows were lowered and her expression angry.

"They wanted me to wear flowers in my hair," she stated accusingly.

"Of course they did," Alissa said pleasantly, moving over to the bed where a number of flowers lay.

Janna walked toward the rigid girl. "Did you hit anyone

with that brush?" she asked, smiling with what she hoped was an infectious smile.

"No!" Rose answered indignantly. "But I threatened to," she admitted.

When Janna chuckled, Rose's hands began to unclench.

"What's the matter?" asked the older woman. She sat on the end of Patrise's bed as if they had all day.

Rose took a deep breath. "I've spent most of my adult life trying to look ugly," she reminded Janna.

"Yes, but you want to change that," Janna reminded her right back.

"I don't want to look ugly anymore," Rose conceded, "but flowers—in my hair?"

"Flowers are lovely in a woman's hair," Alissa said from the bed.

Rose eyed her. Janna had said Alissa was the hair expert. Probably she'd selected what flowers she wanted to use but wasn't sure her target was ready. Rose wasn't sure her target was ready either.

Janna shook her head.

"You are an artist. You embroider flowers all the time. What have you got against having them in your hair?"

"The Yospaldon women wore them in their hair. It's hard for me to copy them. You don't know how hard it is."

"Oh, you've given us a fairly good idea, but flowers don't belong to the Yospaldon women. They belong to the Maker. I think he made them for people to enjoy along with him. I also think he wants us to make things beautiful with them. He made the pastures and meadows beautiful with flowers, didn't he? When we put flowers in a room or on a table or in our hair, we're following his example. You'd better quit embroidering flowers if you don't approve of them, Rose. Maybe we should dig up those bulbs you planted in front of the Girls' Hut. That would take care of those awful Yospaldon women, wouldn't it? It would show them we're not going to copy them, right?"

Janna had a way with words. Rose was smiling by this time, and Alissa made her move.

"Sit here," she ordered, deftly twisting a small piece of wet material around the ends of the trailing vines she had chosen. It would keep them fresh for the evening. She caught up Rose's hair on either side of her face and pinned it over the ends of the vines, hiding the bit of material and letting the loose hair fall back down the sides of Rose's face. The vines fell with the hair. When she was finished, Janna held her breath in delight.

"Alissa, that's beautiful! You've certainly not lost your touch. Go stand in front of the mirror, Rose. You're not the only artist in this room."

Rose crossed the room to the mirror. She stared at herself in growing wonder. A small ruffle of white lace at the neckline accented the dark gray of her dress. Alissa had chosen vines with deep green leaves and tiny white flowers. The green leaves and white flowers mingled with Rose's dark hair, and the overall effect was lovely. Her eyes got big.

"Do you think Benk will like it?" she asked hesitantly.

Janna pounded on Patrise's bed to give her words emphasis. "Yes! He'll fall all over himself liking it—and I intend to be where I can see him fall. Which window will work best?"

"I'll show you," Rose said, motioning them to follow her.

She went into the hall and turned left toward Leftie's room. It had larger windows than most of the other bedrooms and faced the front of the house. The upstairs hallway was quiet, which was a relief after the morning's turmoil; however, both the quiet and the relief were shattered as soon as Rose entered the hall.

"They did it!" yelled Patrise from the bottom of the stairs. "She's wearing flowers in her hair!"

Melona came at a run to see for herself. Janna and Alissa started laughing and Rose did too, though very cautiously. She felt as if she had to hold her head still or the flowers might fall out. It wouldn't be a very relaxed evening, but no one was concerned about that. They were rushing to get into position in front of Leftie's bedroom window.

She followed them and saw that Benk was already outside, standing next to the two horses. Hopefully he hadn't heard any of the fuss. Uh oh, her stomach was starting to feel funny.

Great! It would be just great to get dressed up with flowers in my hair and then burp—or maybe I'll get the hiccups!

"We're ready, Rose. You can go now," Janna told her without turning around.

Rose glared at her friends, huddled eagerly in front of the window. They didn't have anything to burp about; they were having a great time. She was the one who had to go out the front door—but why bother to glare; none of them were looking at her.

She walked back through the hall holding her head in place and descended the stairs, one careful step at a time. With an increasingly funny feeling in her stomach, she left the house and headed towards Benk.

That worthy young man glanced up at the sound of her footsteps, started backwards, and then with an air of deep disgust exclaimed loudly, "What happened to you?"

Rose started smiling, but Benk wasn't through.

"Isn't this a Spring Festival? Why are you wearing dark gray, for high home's sake? Where are the spring colors—and why do you have weeds in your hair?"

A thump came from upstairs in the Girls' Hut as if someone had fallen over. There was an explosion of high-pitched talking. Benk winked at Rose.

"We'd better hurry out of here," he whispered.

"You're in deep trouble," she assured him.

They rode down the street, listening to the ruckus behind them and smiling at each other. Rose had never been happier in her life.

Chapter 14

ANOTHER BIRTH

The Spring Festival wasn't very different from the Fall Festival. The trees and bushes had pale green leaves on them instead of yellow and red ones, but those were the only differences Rose could see. The musicians were playing in a corner like before. Couples were dancing a folk dance to one side of them, while others listened. On the far side of the pasture, people played games in brightly colored tents. Overloaded tables of food in the middle of the pasture could barely be seen for the crowd surrounding them.

Benk and Rose followed the same pattern they'd started at the Fall Festival. First they leaned against a rock and listened to the music. Then they got their food and walked toward Janna's large picnic cloth. It would be a tighter fit this year with Alland's family there, but they'd make room for them, Rose knew. She also knew Benk's time of reckoning had come.

Janna stiffened when she saw him, and a severe expression settled on her face. Her anger had obviously not been dimmed by the intervening hour and a half.

"How dare you say those nasty things about Rose's dress! I promised you'd fall all over yourself when you saw the flowers in her hair, and you insulted her instead; you actually insulted her. No, don't try that innocent act. I know you were performing for the window watchers. I'm not a lamb loony, but I don't think that's any excuse for what you said!"

"Dresses aren't important!" Largen objected loudly.

Tuff wanted to defend his hero too.

"Benk doesn't fall for the girls, Mom. The girls fall for him!"

There was a peal of laughter, and Tuff felt encouraged to say more. "That time Benk took Largen and me to Mount Pasture, you should have seen it. The girls all fell for Benk."

Rose was uncomfortable with the subject and didn't know how to react, but Benk was ready with a comeback.

"Now now, Tuff. Rose is quite different from those other girls. 'Fell for me' isn't what she did the first time we met. 'Smell for me,' is much more accurate!"

Janna's family laughed and Alissa's girls clamored for an explanation. Briefly Rose described her life in Yospaldo and the necessary disguise.

"I've heard this before, but you'll have to tell it again sometime because I want to take notes," Janna said.

"Janna writes things into stories," Benk warned Rose, but she scoffed at the idea of anyone having that much interest in her life.

As quickly as they would allow, she told the group about her escape from Yospaldo. The grownups were mainly interested in the stag and the sheep.

"They must have been the Maker's high home animals!" Janna insisted.

Benk agreed. "They had to be. The stag ran right in front of the wedewolves to lead them away, and the sheep lay on either side of Rose to keep her warm. That's unusual behavior, to say the least."

Janna stared down her nose at him. "Don't talk to me! I'm still angry at you!"

The boys and girls were more captivated with Benk's exploits.

"He made the stream go through the cabin—on the

floor?" Iris asked in wonder.

"Yes," answered Rose patiently. "I thought he was crazy! And yes, Tuff, he used one arrow for each wedewolf."

"Wow!" Tuff and Largen said in unison.

Was it Rose's imagination or did Alland and Petten say "Wow" too under their breaths?

"Oh, that was no big deal," remarked Benk casually.

He was too casual. Both Rose and Janna narrowed their eyes.

Sure enough he continued, "Anybody who knew how to shoot well could have done that. It was a much harder job carrying Rose up the rope ladder. I couldn't breathe through my nose, you see, because the smell—"

"Stop right there, Benk," interrupted Janna. "I know it's hard to change an idea once it gets into your wool-infested brain, but look at Rose. Look at her! Can't you tell a difference between how she was then and how she is now?"

Everyone stared at Rose, who studied the ground in front of her, wishing she could sink into it. *Why did Janna have to say that?*

Benk blinked in astonishment. "Why yes, you're absolutely right. I believe her hair has grown a couple of inches!"

Everyone laughed except Janna who groaned in exasperation. Rose smiled at Benk. He knew her better than anyone else. She could always count on him to relieve a tense situation. Benk grinned at her and then paused with his cup halfway lifted.

"I know how I could get into Janna's good graces again, Rose. Why don't you agree to marry me? I bet that would do it."

Rose tilted her head and gazed off into the distance.

"All right, Benk," she said after a few seconds of distance-gazing. "I'll marry you—to improve your relationship with Janna."

Largen and Tuff gagged, but the girls hugged themselves. It was their first proposal.

Benk started to say something in what Rose could tell would be his most insufferably pompous style. An idea popped into her mind. Leaning over before she lost her nerve, she kissed him right on the lips. Then she sat back, trying to look nonchalant, but her face blushed beyond red into the purple color zone. Benk's lower jaw dropped in utter and complete amazement.

The boys gagged once more, the girls cheered, and the adults alternated between laughing and cheering. Janna laughed heartily, her good humor restored. At long last, Benk's fleece had gotten sheared!

News travels fast in a Montaland kingdom, particularly when its people are enclosed in a pasture. The lines around the game tents were drastically reduced as people queued up to congratulate the newly engaged couple. Rose was hugged by everyone she knew, everyone she didn't know, and then everyone she knew all over again. Her attitude toward crowds of people hadn't changed, and the situation might have had disastrous results if she hadn't been so happy.

"My my my, those flowers in your hair certainly got results," Patrise pointed out when it was her turn.

"Hush, Patrise. Now's not the time," Melona said behind her.

"I predicted this when I met Benk in Yospaldo," Ricaldo bellowed from further down the line, and at his elbow Woofy shouted "Hooray!"

Rose started giggling and couldn't stop. It was out of control and totally out of character. *Methusenakin would be shocked* passed through her mind, but her roommates took it in stride, sympathetically giggling along with her until Benk threatened to throw cold water on the three of them. After that Rose saw one person after another in rapid succession. Ricaldo slowed down the process when he reached her.

"Nurse Broomely would be happy, child," he said in as much of a whisper as he could manage.

She nodded agreement before being engulfed once more

in a merciless stream of huggers. When they were finally able to get on their horses and start through the woods toward the Girls' Hut, Rose was emotionally drained. She stared at the stars, much as she had stared the night of the Fall Festival.

"Well, how was it?"

"How was what?" she hedged though she knew exactly what Benk meant.

"How was it to kiss me?"

He wasn't joking. Rose could hear his uneasiness. She hadn't said a word since they started riding home. He must wonder if she was having second thoughts.

"It was nice."

"Only nice?"

She was too tired to avoid the question. If she and Benk were going to marry, they should start right by being honest with each other.

""I was ugly when I was at Yospaldo. I was dumpy, my face had blotches, I smelled bad, and my hair was greasy. Even so I was grabbed a few times in isolated places and kissed. It was a horrible experience. I hated the feeling of someone's lips pressed against mine. I didn't understand how anybody could enjoy it. The Maker got me away from that place and I've seen a better way of life here, but I didn't think I could ever be normal as far as men were concerned. I didn't think I could ever love one of them."

When she paused for breath, Benk stayed silent, and she knew he was hoping she'd continue.

"When I kissed you, it was nice. I didn't expect it to be, but you're Benk and kissing you wasn't bad. It was nice!"

"'Nice' is good then," Benk said, smiling at her.

Rose smiled back.

"It'll get even better," he promised her.

Two years later a group of women waited in the garden

next to a birthing house, staring at its door.

"This is horrible. It goes beyond horrible. I can't stand it any longer. I'm going to run in there and shake the baby out," Patrise announced.

Melona patted her sister on the back. "You'll be fine. And it's not horrible; it's wonderful."

"Yeah yeah," Patrise muttered, turning to stare at her sister's rounded belly. "Well, I can't go through this again. I let you and Bosky get married, but I withdraw my permission for you to have a baby."

Leftie snorted. "You're being ridiculous, even for you."

"Calm down, everyone," ordered Janna who couldn't stand still and was pacing back and forth.

Something big suddenly appeared at her side and she flinched away, tripped, and fell. Fortunately something else big caught her.

"Any news?" asked Ricaldo.

"No," the women all answered.

"Thanks, Woofy," Janna told the man who had caught her.

"Rosey, she's okay?" asked Woofy.

"I hope so," intoned Patrise in a voice of deep gloom.

"It's Benk who worries me. He was such a nervous wreck last night Windola made him go outside. He was pacing like this little lady here. Back and forth, back and forth," boomed Ricaldo.

"We paced too. Me and Ricado and Benk," Woofy added importantly.

Ricaldo cleared his throat. "We were, uh, keeping him company."

"A pack of pacers," Woofy crowed.

"I'm not a pacer; I'm a collapser," Patrise told them, "and I'm ready to show you how it's done. If that door doesn't open—"

As if on cue the door banged open and Benk staggered into sight.

Everyone jumped. Everyone waited. Several held their breath.

"It's all right. I made it through," he assured them.

Leftie clenched a fist. "Oh, for high home's sake—I'm surrounded by jokers. Give us the news right now or I'll sock you in the stomach."

Benk grinned. "We have a baby girl. Rose is tired but fine."

Pandemonium reigned.

Patrise forgot about collapsing and made up an impromptu dance on the spot. Leftie shrieked joyously. Lifting her arms toward the sky, Melona waved vigorously at a small cloud drifting past. Ricaldo started bellowing a totally unrecognizable song, while Janna and Woofy grabbed each other's hands and spun in a circle.

When they were quiet again, Windola let them in to see Rose and the baby.

"We're calling her Bee after Nurse Broomely. I didn't want to name her anything with broom in it, because Benk would have teased her about sweeping floors the rest of her life. We gave her the old nickname I used to call Nurse B but sort of spread it out to include one of the Maker's little creatures."

Later Patrise gave Rose a painting in celebration of Bee's birth.

"Now don't groan. You haven't even seen it," she scolded as she handed it to the new mother.

Rose was indignant. She'd successfully squelched the groan that had indeed welled up inside her. As she unwrapped the painting, she told Patrise, "Of course I will like it. I will like it because my friend, Patrise, painted it and—oh-h-h!"

There before her was a recognizable meadow with grass. There were recognizable trees around it. The red flowers in the grass were admittedly more like swirls than real flowers, and the yellow dots on the swirls were probably supposed to represent bees, but Rose was impressed.

"You've combined our styles!"

"I figured if you could do it with your tree embroidery, then I could try it too. Do you like it?"

Rose was able to answer honestly. "I do. It has the beauty of a real meadow and trees, and the red swirls and yellow dots give the impression of sunny good cheer."

Melona brightened. "Then you two won't be arguing over art anymore?" she asked hopefully.

Rose and Patrise eyed each other.

"I wouldn't count on it," they said in unison, and all three burst into laughter.

Rose could have sworn she heard someone else laughing too.

The Maker's was the merriest.

The End

About the Author

S . G. (Sally) Byrd grew up in Macon, Georgia, on the Mercer University campus, which she considered her backyard. She graduated from Duke University with a double major in English and Religion. After that, she drove a bookmobile in the beautiful hills of West Virginia, learned to live with Sjogren's syndrome, married, and with her husband Bob, raised three children in Durham, North Carolina—Stephen, Sarah, and Elizabeth.

Making up stories, especially fantasy has always been her gift and delight. *Benk and the Ugly Princess* is the final book in the Montaland series, following *Captives of the Fern Queen* and *Fernpeople*. Sally believes that Christian fantasy has a vital place in today's troubled world.

The Montaland books are fun and entertaining. They are also realistic because they point to a very real God who is loving and powerful and who desires people of all ages to know Him.

Follow Sally at:

www.sgbyrd.com

Facebook: /sgbyrdfantasy

Twitter: @sgbyrdfantasy

Other Books by S.G. Byrd

CAPTIVES OF THE FERN QUEEN

Who wouldn't want to hear about the Stalker—or his daughter, the Fern Queen, who tried to take over Mount Pasture long ago?

And who wouldn't want to meet one of the Maker's high home animals: a blueflame bird whose song is unbearably beautiful, or a lizard whose jewel eggs have amazing healing powers, or a cream colored horse who speaks like a human?

Janna would give anything to get out of her kingdom and see something from the old stories, but when she does get out, it's not exactly what she had in mind. Crawling through a dark tunnel isn't fun and neither is starving as a prisoner of the Fern Queen.

FERNPEOPLE

I n this second book of the Montaland series the evil Fern Queen is dead but five green-veined fernpeople have survived. They will do anything to protect themselves.

The Kingdom of Mount Pasture seems like a peaceful, safe place. The most exciting event in eleven-year-old Benk's life is lambing time. His older brother Alland is traveling to another kingdom to woo a princess. This infuriates Benk who is left behind with pregnant sheep duty.

Sixteen-year-old Janna is baking cookies in Mount Pasture's castle kitchen when something hits her on the head, knocking her to the floor. As she loses consciousness, Janna has a dazed vision of a green-veined arm coming around her and roughly lifting her up. Fernpeople! Fernpeople have her!

Benk "borrows" a horse and sets out from Mount Pasture. Wolves start howling near the fernpeople's hidden cave—and Janna, held hostage, wonders how she can keep going.

CPSIA information can be obtained
at www.ICGtesting.com
Printed in the USA
BVHW072313020221
599232BV00011B/383